"What's on your mind?"

"Remember the idea I told you about?" Lindsey asked.

"You mean for turning the ranch into an event venue?"

"I know what a huge undertaking it would be. So I guess what I'm asking is, would you be willing to help? I'd figure out a way to pay you somehow…eventually…"

"*Pay* me? No, not after—" Booming voices from the kitchen drew Spencer's attention. Sounded like Dad and Tito had just come in. He hated to imagine his grandfather's reaction if he found out what Lindsey was hoping to do next door. "You should go. We can talk about this later."

Mouth flattened, she looked toward the door, then back at Spencer. "It always comes back to the feud, doesn't it? What is wrong with you Navarros that you can't let go of this senseless grudge?"

"Lindsey, please." He stretched one hand toward her.

She backed away, her eyes narrowing. "What was I thinking? You said it yourself twelve years ago—*Navarros and McClements don't mix.*"

Award-winning author **Myra Johnson** writes emotionally gripping stories about love, life and faith. She is a two-time finalist for the ACFW Carol Award and winner of the 2005 RWA Golden Heart® Award. Married since 1972, Myra and her husband have two married daughters and seven grandchildren. She and her husband reside in Texas, sharing their home with two pampered rescue dogs.

Books by Myra Johnson

Love Inspired

The Ranchers of Gabriel Bend

The Rancher's Family Secret

Rancher for the Holidays
Her Hill Country Cowboy
Hill Country Reunion
The Rancher's Redemption
Their Christmas Prayer

Visit the Author Profile page at Harlequin.com.

The Rancher's Family Secret

Myra Johnson

LOVE INSPIRED

INSPIRATIONAL ROMANCE

LOVE INSPIRED®

INSPIRATIONAL ROMANCE

Recycling programs for this product may not exist in your area.

ISBN-13: 978-1-335-48862-6

The Rancher's Family Secret

Love Inspired
22 Adelaide St. West, 40th Floor
Toronto, Ontario M5H 4E3, Canada
www.Harlequin.com

Printed in U.S.A.

Let all bitterness, and wrath, and anger, and clamour, and evil speaking, be put away from you, with all malice: And be ye kind one to another, tenderhearted, forgiving one another, even as God for Christ's sake hath forgiven you.
—*Ephesians* 4:31–32

The best part about moving home to Texas in 2019 has been rekindling ties with extended family. To my dear loved ones, though the busyness of our separate lives means we can't always spend as much time together as we'd like, just knowing you're near brings me joy and sets my heart at ease. I'm so grateful to have each one of you in my life.

Special thanks to my niece Lois for sharing insights from her "adventures" in developing their beautiful New Mexico property as an event venue! I also want to give a big shout-out to my longtime friend and fellow Love Inspired author Tina Radcliffe, who helped me shape my early ideas for this story; to my tireless editor, Melissa Endlich, for her wise and gentle guidance; to Natasha Kern, the best agent a writer could ever hope for; and to my devoted husband and daughters, whose love, prayers and encouragement never fail to lift me up when the going gets tough!

Chapter One

"Aunt Audra!" Lindsey McClement burst from her car to envelop her favorite aunt in a bear hug. Feeling the bony shoulders and xylophone-like ribs beneath Audra's cable-knit sweater, she tried not to visibly react.

Audra returned the embrace with a mighty one of her own. "Oh, honey, you're a grown woman now. I'm not *that* much older than you, so why don't we just drop the *aunt*?" With tears in her eyes, she laughed as she held Lindsey at arm's length. "I'm so glad you're here. You're even prettier than ever. Your hair's so much longer than when I last saw you."

Groaning, Lindsey shoved a tangle of dark curls off her shoulder. "And still as unmanageable as ever."

"No, it's beautiful. You definitely inherited the family's 'good hair' genes—which totally bypassed me." Audra pinned a limp brown strand into her messy bun before turning toward the back of the car. "Let me help with your luggage."

"It's okay, I've got it." Lindsey hurried to grab one of the larger suitcases out of the trunk. Her aunt, once strong and vibrant, didn't appear capable of lifting much of anything. New streaks of silver in her hair only underscored this courageous woman's struggles. She and her husband, Charles Forrester, had managed the McClement ranch for Lindsey's grandparents for many years, taking over completely after both elder McClements had passed away. Then at the end of August, Uncle Charles, an army veteran partially paralyzed by an IED while serving in Iraq, had succumbed to a lengthy illness. Lindsey's chest ached at the thought of Audra striving to carry on alone.

Not to be deterred, her aunt hefted one of the bags, then led the way up the broad porch steps. "I've got your room ready—the one you always liked in the summer because of the shade from the red oak."

"I remember when the tree was only a sapling." Lindsey paused on the top step. The elegant whitewashed Central Texas farmhouse she'd visited so often throughout her childhood looked the same…and yet not. Time and neglect had taken their toll.

"I know what you're thinking." Audra sighed as they walked into the wide foyer. "Since Charles—" A small choking noise sounded in her throat. "I haven't had the will or the wherewithal to keep up this place. I've already sold off most of the herd to keep from going completely under."

"It's okay. I'm here to help." Lindsey gave her aunt a gentle squeeze. "It's time someone took care of *you* for a change." Audra's dismissive wave couldn't hide the moisture filling her eyes.

Jaw clenched, she hefted Lindsey's suitcase and marched up the curving carpeted staircase. "Don't know what I'd have done the last few months if not for

Spencer pitching in—though his dad and grandpa most likely don't approve."

At the mention of Spencer Navarro, Lindsey's heart threw in an extra beat. As a young teenager, she'd harbored a major crush on the ebony-haired, dashingly good-looking boy whose family owned the neighboring horse ranch. Didn't matter that his identical twin brother, Samuel, was the more outgoing and fun-loving of the two. Something about Spencer's quiet nature and gentle way with horses had enthralled her from the first time they'd met.

That is, until the summer after her seventeenth birthday, when he'd cruelly broken her heart. Humiliating her in front of all his friends at the Gabriel Bend Fourth of July picnic, he'd stated loudly enough for everyone to hear, "Beat it, Lindsey. Navarros and McClements don't mix."

Shaking off the memory, she rolled her suitcase to the end of the four-poster bed. "Does Spencer still have the beard?" It had been a new look for him when she'd glanced his way at Uncle Charles's funeral. At least he and his mother had had the courtesy to show up and pay their respects, even if his father and grandfather couldn't put aside the long-standing Navarro-McClement feud long enough to do so themselves.

"The beard's a nice change. Manly, don't you think?" Audra patted Lindsey's arm. "Let's get the rest of your things upstairs. Then you can freshen up while I get supper on the table."

"I'm fine, Aunt—I mean, Audra. Really, I don't want you fussing over me."

"But this is your first night here, and you've had such a long drive from St. Louis." Already bustling toward the door, Audra turned with a bright smile. "I'm cooking your favorite—pot roast with new potatoes, peas and baby carrots."

"I can smell it already." Lindsey inhaled appreciatively, then linked arms with her aunt. "The rest of my things can wait till morning. Tell me what I can do to help you in the kitchen, and then we can sit down for a nice, long chat over supper."

Predictably, Audra refused to let Lindsey lift a finger while she bustled around the kitchen setting out dishes and flatware, filling glasses with iced tea, and tossing a garden salad. A glance at the built-in desk next to the fridge revealed a chaotic stack of paperwork—mostly bills, judging from what Lindsey could see from where she sat. Would her aunt think her too forward if she took a closer look? It was part of the reason she'd come after all—to try to make sense of her aunt's financial nightmare in the wake of Uncle Charles's illness and death.

Before she could act on the impulse, a knock sounded at the back door. "Would you get that, honey?" Audra paused in the middle of transferring the pot roast and veggies to a platter. "It's probably Spencer. The sweet boy brings me my mail sometimes so I don't have to trek all the way down to the road."

The hitch in Lindsey's heartbeat returned. She rose stiffly, then tugged at her jeans and sweater on her way to the door. Opening it, she pasted on a cool smile for the man in the denim jacket and cowboy hat. "Spencer. Long time no see."

Dark brows shot up over eyes the color of richest sable. "Lindsey?" Her name came out in a surprised squeak. "Didn't realize the strange car out front was yours."

"The Missouri plates weren't a dead giveaway?" Seeing him again up close—and with the neatly trimmed facial hair making him look even more rakishly handsome than she remembered—it was all she could do to keep her tone casual.

"Guess I wasn't paying attention." He tapped a stack of envelopes and advertising flyers against his palm. "I brought Audra's mail."

"Thank you." She swallowed. "I hear you've been kind to my aunt."

"Just being neighborly." Handing her the mail, he nodded and turned to go.

Audra joined Lindsey at the door. "Spencer, maybe you could help Lindsey bring in the rest of her luggage."

"Uh, sure. Anything I can do."

"I told you it can wait." Lindsey flicked her hand in a dismissive gesture. "I'm sure Spencer has better things to do, and we were about to eat, so—"

"Go on, honey." Audra winked as she reached for the mail Lindsey held. "I'll keep supper warm. And you're certainly welcome to stay and join us, Spencer."

"Thank you, ma'am, but my mom already has something in the oven."

"Another time, then. Lindsey's going to be here a good long while, so you two will have lots of time to catch up." With a satisfied nod, Audra returned to her meal preparations.

Lindsey folded her arms in a vain attempt to quell the awkwardness of the moment. "It's fine if you need to get home, Spencer."

He looked almost ready to take her up on the reprieve. Then, with a barely disguised sigh, he said, "No rush. Mom doesn't usually serve dinner until closer to seven."

"If you're sure—"

"I wouldn't have offered if I wasn't."

"But you didn't offer. Aunt Audra volunteered you."

"Semantics," he said with a sharp laugh. "Want to stand here arguing about it or shall we get the job done?"

She flinched. "I'll grab my keys."

Amazing good looks included, Spencer Navarro hadn't changed much over the years. Seemed his easy rapport with horses had never transitioned to effective people skills.

Either that, or he found Lindsey's presence even more offensive than he had twelve years ago.

Open mouth, insert foot. The story of Spencer's life. It was obvious Lindsey hadn't forgotten his teenage stupidity. Hadn't forgiven him, either.

Clamping his teeth together, he marched around the side of the house to where Lindsey had parked. Did the woman have any clue how badly she intimidated him? Smart, classy Lindsey McClement could do no wrong in his eyes, but he couldn't seem to do anything right in hers. Hence, the fateful moment when he'd snubbed her in front of all his friends because…well, he hadn't really had a good reason, except that a group of his grandfather's cronies had been watching from across the street. Although Dad and Tito—short for *abuelito*, the Spanish word for "grandpa"—usually turned a blind eye to the twins and Lindsey hanging out together on the ranch, fraternizing with a McClement in public wasn't so easily tolerated.

The front porch light blinked on, and Lindsey trotted

down the steps. Keys in hand, she popped the trunk. "If you wouldn't mind getting the heavier suitcases, I'd appreciate it."

He stared wide-eyed at the array of luggage, bags and boxes. "Wow, looks like you're moving in."

"I am, actually…for now." She edged around him to scoop up a couple of bulging shopping bags.

"But I thought you had a great job at some big financial firm in St. Louis."

"*Had* being the operative word. I quit last week. And the job wasn't that great."

He'd obviously hit on a sore subject. "Sorry." Unsure what else to say, he manhandled a two-ton suitcase out of the trunk, then tromped inside behind Lindsey.

Upstairs, they followed a threadbare carpet runner down the long hallway. At the far door, Lindsey showed him into an airy but cluttered guest room. The branches of a scraggly oak tree clawed the window screen.

"Anywhere's fine," Lindsey said, motioning toward the monster suitcase pulling his shoulder out of its socket. "I'll figure out later where everything will go."

He maneuvered the behemoth over to a mirrored armoire. "Forgot how big this house is. A lot to manage for someone living alone, not to mention trying to keep the ranch going."

"We'll find a way. There's been a McClement living in this house since my grandpa settled here more than sixty-five years ago." Almost to herself, she added, "And if I have any say in the matter, that isn't going to change."

Spencer didn't risk a reply. No sense bringing up how his grandfather and Lindsey's had once been best friends and together had invested in the original ranch holdings, now split down the middle by a couple miles of barbed-wire fence.

More importantly, he couldn't imagine why Audra Forrester would want to stay on here by herself. She and Charles had moved in nearly twenty years ago so her parents could age in place. The elder McClements had since passed on, and it had been just Audra and Charles puttering around in the huge old house while struggling to keep the family cattle business going. Even with Charles coming home from Iraq a paraplegic, they'd both been determined to carry on. Somehow they'd made it work. Feuding families or not, Spencer couldn't help but admire such courage.

A year ago Charles had gotten sick with the flu, which had turned into pneumonia, and his lungs never fully recovered. He'd had one infection after another, and when he caught a cold a few months ago, it proved too much for his weakened system. The sight of Lindsey comforting her weeping aunt at the graveside, Charles's wheelchair standing empty nearby, had almost done Spencer in. Considering his and Lindsey's history, any words of sympathy he'd hoped to offer would have come out sounding useless and hollow, so he'd left that duty to his much more tactful mother and quietly slipped away.

Of course, if Audra did sell the property, Lindsey would have no more reason to visit Gabriel Bend. Not that he'd seen her that often the past several years. Following his public rebuff, those lengthy summer vacations at her grandparents' ranch had come to an abrupt end. He'd heard she'd gone on to a prestigious college, then accepted the allegedly not-so-great job in St. Louis. Charles Forrester's funeral was the first time in years that Spencer could remember her being in town for more than a couple of days at a time.

They made two more treks upstairs without much more than an "Excuse me" or an "Oops" as they tried not to get in each other's way. After the final trip, Spencer paused in the foyer, hand on the doorknob. "It's good you're here. For your aunt's sake. She's had a rough time."

"Yes, she has." Mouth firm, Lindsey glanced away. "I'm grateful for how good you've been to Aunt Audra since Uncle Charles died. But I'm here now, so…"

"Right." He pulled open the door. "I'll stay out of your way."

"I didn't mean it like that, Spencer." Arms crossed, she released a slow breath. "It's just that…since we're likely to cross paths now and again… I don't want things to be awkward between us."

"It's okay. I get it."

"Good. Thank you for understanding. And thanks again for helping with my stuff." She rested a hand on the side of the door, preparing to close it behind him. "Say hi to your mother for me."

"Sure. You, too." Striding out to the porch, he rolled his eyes at his lame reply. *Good one, Navarro. Articulate as ever.* His brother, a successful commercial real estate broker in Houston, would have had no trouble coming back with something charming and witty.

Or could this be Spencer's chance to offer a long-overdue apology?

He halted and turned slightly, fingertips stuffed into his back pockets. "Lindsey, I wanted to say I'm sorry about—"

"Hey, looks like you've got company." She leaned in the open doorway.

He looked toward the road, where a mud-encrusted sheriff's department SUV pulling a two-horse trailer passed through his entrance gate. The trailer rode too heavy to be empty. "Better get home. Looks like the livestock deputy's delivering the rescue horse he called me about."

"A rescue?" Lindsey's brows drew together.

"Yeah, the deputy sometimes calls on me to foster a horse until it's healthy enough be rehomed—when my dad allows it, anyway." Frustration gnawing, Spencer frowned. "He's concerned about something contagious being spread to our quarter horses."

"I can see how that might be a problem." Lower lip drawn between her teeth, Lindsey studied him. Her gaze softened. "Your love of horses—it's one of the things I always most admired about you."

He swallowed his surprise. "Thanks. I didn't think—"

"You should go." She nodded toward his driveway, where the deputy was unloading a horse from the back of the trailer.

"Right. See you around." Before this conversation became even more uncomfortable, he jogged down the steps and headed across the field toward home.

And thought about Lindsey the whole way, back when they were innocent kids who couldn't have cared less about a stupid family feud. He'd once thought of Lindsey as just a city kid having fun playing cowgirl for a few weeks every summer. Until they were teens, anyway, when he'd started seeing her in a whole new way. Then, watching his much more outgoing twin flirt with her, he'd accepted that he could never compete with Samuel's charisma.

Sam. Right. Which might be the true reason he'd so callously brushed her off that summer. He loved his brother, but it sure was hard sometimes living in Samuel's shadow.

Watching Spencer go, Lindsey suffered a shiver of disappointment. A part of her wished she'd offered to help Spencer with the rescue horse. As a kid, she'd spent many steamy summer mornings working alongside the Navarro boys as they mucked stalls and groomed horses. Samuel had typically hurried through chores so he could do something fun. Perhaps it was Spencer's thoughtful way of making sure everything was done right that had first captured her heart. After chores, when the three of them would saddle up to go gallivanting across the pastures in search of adventure, she'd try to stick close to him, though he'd never seemed to return her interest. Too bad she hadn't gotten the message.

Even so, Lindsey's summers in Gabriel Bend remained among her happiest vacation memories. In fact, after her parents separated the year she'd turned twelve, those weeks spent at the McClement ranch had become her lifeline.

Stomach clenching, she went inside and quietly closed the door. Everything had changed after Dad walked out. Mom had been a total wreck, and if Audra hadn't taken Mom's side instead of her selfish brother's, things would have been even harder.

"Lindsey," Audra called from the kitchen, "supper's ready whenever you are."

"Coming." Suppressing a surge of bitterness toward

her traitorous father, she strode down the hall. Perhaps someday she could forgive him for turning his back on the family, but it hadn't happened yet. If he'd shown even the slightest remorse—but no, he seemed perfectly content living somewhere near Tulsa with his current live-in girlfriend and her two kids from her own failed marriage. Guess they deserved each other.

Audra was ladling gravy into a deep-sided bowl. "Haven't heard so much tromping up and down that creaky staircase since you and your mom used to come for summer vacations." She chuckled. "How many trips to your car did it take?"

Lindsey narrowed one eye in thought as she took her chair. "Three or four? I lost count. But I'm sure my quads will remind me in the morning."

"Nice that Spencer could spare a few minutes to give you a hand. He's such a sweetheart." Finger to her chin, Audra surveyed the table. "Did I forget anything? I have artificial sweetener if you'd prefer."

Lindsey seized her aunt's hand and cast her a chiding smile. "Everything is fine. Sit down right now and stop fussing."

Giving a weak laugh, Audra obeyed but frowned as if it pained her not to be doing something more. Her compliance lasted about five minutes before she hopped up to add more ice to Lindsey's glass, then a few minutes later to refill the gravy bowl. The dear woman didn't know how to stop taking care of others and just *be*.

After supper, Lindsey put her foot down. "*I* am doing the dishes, and if you move from that chair, I will escort you from the kitchen and bolt the door."

Audra feigned a pout. "Can I disobey long enough to give you a hug?"

"Fine," Lindsey said, rising, "but stay in your chair and I'll come around to you."

As they shared the embrace, she noted again her aunt's gaunt frame. Though Audra had served herself an ample portion of pot roast, far too much remained on her plate. Lindsey briefly debated whether to mention her concern but decided it could wait. After a few days of combing through Audra's financial mess, perhaps she could relieve her aunt's worries enough that she'd relax and start eating better.

It was a challenge keeping Audra from bobbing up and down to show Lindsey where to find containers for leftovers, dishcloths, a scouring pad and dish drainer. She finally relented and allowed her aunt to move her chair closer to the sink so they could chat while Lindsey washed dishes.

"I still can't believe Grandma and Grandpa went all those years without a dishwasher." Lindsey grinned over her shoulder. "You, either, for that matter."

"The house is too old. We'd have to tear out some cabinets, redo the plumbing...not worth the hassle."

"But it's a huge kitchen. You'd lose very little cupboard space, and only right here by the sink."

"Charles always said the same thing. Said if we had the kitchen remodeled to be more wheelchair-friendly, he'd take over the cooking and cleanup." Audra heaved a mournful sigh, then dabbed her eyes with her sweater sleeve. "He would have done anything for me."

"He was a wonderful man." With fond memories of her uncle parading through her thoughts, Lindsey scrubbed another plate and rinsed it under the faucet. As she set it in the drainer, her gaze drifted beyond the window.

Though darkness had fallen, vapor lights at the Navarro ranch lit the gravel lane and the area outside the nearest barn. The SUV and horse trailer were still parked there, and Spencer appeared to be in deep conversation with the deputy. Spencer gestured toward the barn, then gave the man a firm handshake. They must have come to some agreement about fostering the horse.

Apparently forgetting her promise to stay seated, Audra stood and joined Lindsey at the sink. "Spying on our handsome neighbor, I see. Wondered why you suddenly got quiet."

"I wasn't spying. I just—" Pointless to deny the truth, although she preferred *neighborly interest* to *spying.*

"Oh, looks like Deputy Miller brought him another rescue horse. He must get one or two new ones every month or so. Can't turn 'em away."

Lindsey cast her aunt a knowing smile. "Remind you of anyone?"

"If you're referring to my penchant for taking in homeless favorite nieces, then I plead guilty as charged."

"I wasn't exactly homeless, you know." Lindsey set the last of the cooking pots in the drainer, then dried her hands.

"Well, you weren't planning on staying in St. Louis after quitting your job, were you?" Squaring off with Lindsey, Audra shook a finger in her face. "And if I ever find out the only reason you quit your job was so you'd be free to come help me—"

"Absolutely not. I'd been thinking for months about leaving the company but hadn't come up with strong enough motivation. I have you to thank for nudging me off dead center. And while we're getting your finances back on solid ground, I'll have plenty of time to figure out what I want to do next."

"Or…you could stay with me and find a suitable but stress-free job right here in Gabriel Bend." Audra gathered a handful of flatware from the drainer and began sorting it into a drawer. "That's what I'm praying for, anyway."

After all her aunt had been through, she still believed God heard her prayers? Lindsey shook her head. "Not sure I have that kind of faith anymore."

"Oh, honey, if you're sure, then it isn't faith." Closing the drawer, Audra slid an arm around Lindsey's waist and smiled at their dim reflection in the window glass. "Anyway, I've got enough for both of us. God answered my prayer by bringing you here, didn't He? So I'm confident He'll take care of the rest."

Despite her faith struggles, Lindsey couldn't deny a sense of spiritual intervention in her decision to leave her dead-end job and come to Gabriel Bend. She only hoped God would show her a way to keep Audra on the ranch she loved. Yes, it was entirely too much for one person—or even two—to manage. Not to mention Lindsey's ranching knowledge was limited to watching over the fence or from the back of a pickup as her grandpa and aunt tended the cattle. Even after his disability, Uncle Charles had done his part, too, either from horseback in a specially designed saddle or pulling a hay-filled trailer behind the ranch's army-green Kawasaki Mule. Charles had also been the one with the most business sense. Bereft of his wise fiscal management, it was no wonder Audra's growing debts had pushed her close to bankruptcy in recent months.

But this ranch was the family legacy, and Lindsey's

heart clenched to think how close her aunt was to losing it. There was a lot of rebuilding to do, but perhaps once she cleared up Audra's financial situation, she could hire reliable help for her aunt to keep the ranch going.

Spencer, perhaps? He'd already been pitching in. If his grandfather, grouchy old Arturo Navarro, would only get past whatever ridiculous grudge he continued to harbor against Lindsey's late grandfather, the possibility might be worth exploring…

But not tonight. It was all too much to think about right now. After two days on the road and a meal of her favorite comfort food, she could barely keep her eyes open. "I think the trip is catching up with me. Mind if I turn in early?"

"Not at all. I'm sure you're exhausted."

Lindsey kissed her aunt's cheek. "You get a good night's rest, too. We can start looking over your finances first thing in the morning."

Chapter Two

Stepping out the back door into a cold and gloomy December dawn, Spencer zipped his down vest and tugged the brim of his dusty brown Stetson. Chores began early at the ranch, and the first thing he needed to do was look in on the new arrival. The sorrel mare was badly undernourished. To make matters worse, sores covered her rump where some ignorant kid had peppered her with a pellet gun.

What was wrong with people who took morbid pleasure in inflicting pain upon an innocent animal? Spencer would give almost anything to get his hands on the creep and teach him a thing or two.

In the smaller barn where he isolated his rescue horses, he grabbed the equine first aid kit and sidled into the stall. "Easy, there, Cinnamon." Deputy Miller didn't have information about the horse's name, so Spencer had decided to call her Cinnamon because of the deep red in her coat. He stroked her neck. "Don't worry, girl. I'm going to take good care of you."

She flinched a few times as he tended her wounds, but she had a gentle spirit and seemed to understand she was in a safe place. When he finished, he freshened her water pail and offered a small portion of easily digestible horse feed. The vet would be out soon to evaluate her and advise him about a nutritional plan.

As he lathered his hands at the wash station, his father strode into the barn. "How is the mare? Will she recover?"

"Think so. It'll take time, though."

His father grunted. "And money. I know the county pays you a stipend, but we're running a quarter horse business here, not a charitable operation. If you intend to continue taking in rescues, you'd better come up with a plan for covering the extra expense—*and* somewhere else to keep them besides this ranch."

"I'm working on it." Spencer struggled to curb his irritation over his father's continual grumbling about the rescue horses. Problem was, he *hadn't* given enough thought to the cost of his efforts. The livestock deputy had suggested he look into registering as a nonprofit equine rescue program so he could solicit donations and move into a dedicated rescue facility, but his ranch responsibilities had kept him too busy to do so.

"Perhaps you should talk to Lindsey since she's back in town. She has a finance degree, right?" His father harrumphed. "Something you should have thought about before quitting college. Your brother at least went on to make something of himself." Under his breath, he added, "Even if he did turn his back on the family business."

"I'm here, aren't I?" Indignation twisted Spencer's gut. "Can't you give me credit for that much?"

"Credit is all I've given you since you decided to take in so many starving and abused horses. Your grandfather and I have invested too much in our quarter horse breeding program to have you ruin it by introducing strangles or some other disease into the herd."

"I quarantine each new arrival until it gets a clean bill of health. As long as we keep our herd's vaccinations up-to-date, you have nothing to worry about." Jaw clenched, Spencer slapped on his Stetson. "Excuse me while I get on with my work."

"And when you're through tending to your charity case, perhaps you can spare a few minutes to help me with the horses that actually earn their keep." His father stormed out.

Enrique "Hank" Navarro was a hard man to please, and Spencer wondered sometimes why he kept trying. Perhaps because his father was one of the wisest and most accomplished horsemen he'd ever known. Everything Spencer knew about horses he'd learned from working alongside his father and grandfather since he and his brother were old enough to toddle around in boots and pint-size cowboy hats. But since he'd begun putting his hard-earned equine knowledge to work on his own terms, he couldn't seem to earn either Dad's or Tito's respect.

Perhaps he should have finished college. If he had an equine management degree to hang on the wall, Dad might show a little more pride in his son. Not that school could have taught him much more than what he'd absorbed from hands-on experience here at the ranch.

Except…if he'd stuck it out, he could have added a few classes in accounting and budgeting.

Maybe Dad had a point. Lindsey had the financial know-how Spencer lacked, and now she was living next door. But did he dare bother her for advice when she had so much to deal with concerning her aunt's situation?

Besides, there was still the matter of the apology he hadn't found the nerve or opportunity to offer.

By midmorning he'd cleaned stalls in the small barn where he stabled the rescues and the main quarter horse barn. The vet came by and noted that Cinnamon's most concerning issues appeared to be the pellet gun wounds and malnutrition. He took blood samples and said the results would be back in a couple of days.

"About the bill," Spencer began. He glanced toward the arena where his father was starting a young mare under saddle. "Can you make sure it's addressed directly to me and not to Navarro Quarter Horses?"

The vet offered an understanding nod. "Come by the clinic next time you're in town and we'll settle up then."

The next few days kept him jumping back and forth between tending to Cinnamon's injuries and keeping his father placated by putting in extra time with the quarter horses. With several broodmares expecting to foal next spring, it never hurt to get an early start preparing birthing stalls and ensuring all the necessary supplies were on hand.

Returning from the farm supply store on Friday, Spencer looked over to see Lindsey making her way across the field. Dressed in a pink turtleneck peeking out from beneath an oversize plaid flannel shirt, and with her dark brown curls cascading from a ponytail, she looked like a fashion model from one of his mom's country living magazines.

"Hi," she called with a tentative wave. Halting just short of the barbed-wire fence separating the Mc-Clement and Navarro properties, she held out something loaf-shaped wrapped in foil with a red bow on top. "Audra's been baking. She sent me over with this as a small thank-you for your kindness these past few months. It's her holiday pumpkin bread."

A treat Spencer had enjoyed many times over the years. Already mentally savoring the delicious mix of pumpkin, spices and chopped walnuts, he strode toward the fence. "Wow, thanks."

Carefully avoiding the top strand of barbed wire, Lindsey passed over the loaf. "Did everything work out with the rescue horse?"

"Yeah, looks like she'll be fine." He surprised himself with the next words out of his mouth. "Would you like to meet her?"

A flicker of interest brightened Lindsey's eyes. "Would that be okay?"

"Of course." His thermal Henley and down vest had felt perfectly comfortable all morning. Why did he suddenly feel like he was roasting? He nodded down the fence line toward the spot where, as kids, they'd separated the wire strands with two sturdy cedar branches so they could pass back and forth without getting snagged by the barbs.

Weaving around gnarled cedar trees and underbrush, they reached the opening at the same time. With Spencer standing across from her, Lindsey touched one of the dried-out gray limbs. "You left the fence propped open all these years?"

"Guess I always thought…hoped…" He stared hard at the bow atop the pumpkin bread. "Lindsey, what I said that day… I didn't mean it. I was an ignorant kid. I'm sorry."

For several unbearable moments she didn't reply. Then, "You ruined my entire summer, you know."

Her softly spoken words lasered straight through his chest. He met her gaze with all the sincerity he could muster. "If I could take it all back, I'd do it in a heartbeat."

She released a harsh sigh. "Stupid feud."

"Yeah, stupid." Yet his grandfather still wouldn't let it go. To this day, Spencer wasn't clear on what had come between Arturo Navarro and Egan McClement all those years ago. Now this ugly barbed-wire fence severed what had once been Rancho de Manos y Corazón—Hands and Heart Ranch—the vision of two army buddies who'd become best friends while serving in the Korean War.

It was all Tito talked about most days, his unrelenting desire to reclaim the land Egan "stole" from him when the partnership splintered and they legally divided the ranch and holdings. Now that Charles Forrester had passed way, Tito was convinced Audra would finally decide to sell, and he intended to win the bid.

"So," Lindsey said, pulling his thoughts to the present, "are you going to show me your rescue horse or not?"

"Sure." With the pumpkin bread tucked under one arm, Spencer braced the fence opening while Lindsey bent to ease through.

Stepping out on the Navarro side, she straightened with a groan. "Seemed a lot easier when we were kids. Don't tell me you still use this when you go back and forth to Audra's?"

"Not anymore. Sometimes I go around by the road, but usually I climb over at one of the fence posts."

Lindsey glanced back at the opening, a sad smile creasing her lips. "Guess we've both outgrown the past."

Unsure if that was an entirely good thing, Spencer merely nodded and started toward the barn.

Catching up, Lindsey asked, "What's the story about this horse?"

"The deputy told me he found her near Liberty Hill. Said the owner's losing his farm and couldn't afford the feed bills. Plus, he had to keep chasing off a bored kid with a pellet gun."

"Oh, no! The horse was shot?"

Spencer gave a grim nod as they entered the barn. After leaving the pumpkin bread on a nearby shelf, he led the way to Cinnamon's stall. "Don't be put off by how bad she looks. The wounds will heal, and after a few weeks of good nutrition, she'll be a fine little mare."

"Poor thing." Lindsey held out her hand, and the mare ambled over for a scratch beneath her chin. "She's so friendly."

"And forgiving, despite what she's been through."

"Easier said than done. For some of us, anyway." With a tired exhalation, she folded her arms along the top of the stall gate. "I've been spending nearly every waking hour since I got here trying to sort out Audra's financial mess, and this morning I got upset with my dad again for how he's abdicated any responsibility for his share of the ranch."

Spencer couldn't forget how angry and withdrawn she'd been the first summer after her father had skipped out on them. He hated seeing Lindsey so troubled, and no response he could think of seemed adequate. Why was it so easy to tell her all about his horses and so hard to talk about anything more personal?

He reached for the halter and lead rope hanging from the gate. "I need to take Cinnamon out for a short walk to give her some exercise. You're welcome to come along."

Being around Spencer again was bringing back all kinds of memories—mostly good ones, but others...not so much. She'd devolved into a total mess the summer Dad left. At an awkward stage between childhood and adolescence, she'd been angry one minute, sulky the next, and generally an absolute grouch.

But Spencer had shown her more understanding than anyone. He hadn't tried to talk her off her metaphorical ledges or commiserated with her about what a louse her father had turned out to be. He was simply there. He'd let her muck stalls with him while his wild and reckless twin brother jumped out of the hayloft, or he'd saddle a couple of horses and lead her on a trail ride through the pastures. She surmised Spencer was only thinking up things to do that would keep her out of trouble, but by the end of the summer, she'd fallen head over heels in puppy love with him.

She cringed at the warmth creeping up her face. When Spencer handed her Cinnamon's lead rope, she figured this was another of his attempts to find something "safe" he could occupy her with.

"We won't go far," he said, walking beside her. "She needs to gradually build up her strength as she regains some weight."

Lindsey reached up to caress Cinnamon's cheek. "Such a sweetie. How long before her wounds heal?"

"They're mostly on the surface, so a couple of weeks, provided there's no infection. With daily saline rinses and antibiotic ointment, she should be fine." They'd reached a small paddock. Spencer unlatched the gate and motioned her through. "Once around the perimeter and we'll head back. Don't want to tire her out too much."

The midday sun, peeping out from behind the clouds, stole some of the chill from the December air. Lindsey tilted her head to receive the golden rays. "This is so much better than spending fifty hours a week in a stuffy, windowless cubicle."

"So you really quit your job?"

"I really did."

Spencer gave a thoughtful nod, and they continued in silence for several steps until he asked, "What now? I mean, will you apply somewhere else, or…?"

"Haven't thought that far ahead. I have some savings to fall back on, so I plan to stay and help Audra as long as she needs me." Releasing a tired laugh, she let her head fall forward. "And judging from the avalanche of bills and insurance paperwork I've been digging through, the end is nowhere in sight."

"Sounds like you have plenty to keep you busy."

She narrowed her eyes at him. Was this a subtle hint for her to leave? "If I'm keeping you from something—"

"No, didn't mean it like that." Tucking his fingers into his vest pockets, Spencer uttered a nervous laugh. "I…uh…was wondering…"

She angled a wary glance his way. "Wondering what?"

They'd circled back to the gate. Spencer held it open while Lindsey led the horse through, then latched it behind her. "See, taking in rescue horses can get expensive, and I thought with your financial know-how, maybe you could give me some advice."

He actually wanted her help? "What kind of advice are you looking for—budgeting, bookkeeping, cash flow management?"

"All of the above. It's either that—" he glared toward the barn "—or risk my dad putting his foot down about fostering more rescues."

"I would have thought your father, of all people, would be in favor of saving horses' lives."

"In principle, yes. But not if it cuts into the quarter horse business." Spencer's frown indicated the issue had been eating at him awhile. Back in the barn, he released Cinnamon into her stall, then pointed toward the sink. "We need to wash up. Can't risk spreading infection."

While they took turns scrubbing their hands with potent-smelling disinfectant soap, Lindsey pondered Spencer's request. "Have you considered forming a non-profit and raising funds that way?"

"Deputy Miller suggested the same thing." Drying his hands, Spencer shrugged. "But it sounds more complicated than I have time to figure out."

Lindsey nodded thoughtfully as she accepted the clean towel Spencer offered. "I can look into it for you."

"If it means taking time away from your aunt's affairs—"

"Honestly, it'd be a welcome break." She propped her hips against the wall. "Wouldn't share this with just anyone, but I'm going a little bit crazy over there. The condition of Audra's finances is not a pretty picture."

"It's clear she's been struggling since Charles died." Spencer dropped their used towels into a hamper. "I've asked several times if I could do more for her—feed her livestock, make minor repairs, whatever she needed. But your aunt is…" He glanced away, brows knit as if he searched for the right words.

"A difficult woman to help." Lindsey nodded. "Believe me, I get it. She doesn't know how to stop doing for others and let someone else take care of her."

"What's she going to do, then? To support herself."

Eyes narrowed, Lindsey hiked her chin. "I can promise you one thing—she *isn't* selling the McClement ranch." Her confidence wavered, and she pressed her palms against her temples. "Except I have no idea yet how to keep that from happening."

"If anyone can…" Spencer roughly cleared his throat. "On the other hand, a widow running a cattle ranch all on her own? If there happened to be an interested buyer— "

"There has to be another solution. I'm not giving up." Lips pursed, she studied him. "Can I bounce an idea off you?"

"Uh, sure."

She meandered outside and gazed toward her aunt's house. "I keep remembering the thrill I felt each summer when Mom turned up the lane—the pristine white farmhouse surrounded by a lush green lawn, Grandma's rosebushes bordering the porch, cattle grazing in the grassy pastures. And the little family chapel—remember when we used to sneak in there and play church?"

"Hard to forget my brother's rambling 'sermons'—or the time your grandmother caught us in there and gave us what for."

"Grandma was so sure the hundred-year-old building would come crashing down with the next gust of wind. And yet it's still standing." Lindsey snickered.

"Although possibly only because the junk stored in there is holding up the walls."

"I don't know," Spencer mused with a crooked smile. "Some things are built to last."

Like childhood friendships, perhaps? Lindsey ducked her head before Spencer could glimpse the blush warming her face. "Anyway," she continued in a rush, "I started thinking the ranch would make a great location as a photography setting or even a country wedding venue. We'd need to do major cleanup and repairs, but can you see the potential? Or am I only grasping at straws?"

The smile left Spencer's face. "If Audra's already so deeply in debt, how can she afford to turn the property into a wedding venue?"

"That's what I keep coming back to." Shoulders sagging, Lindsey exhaled a weary sigh. "I should get back. You have things to do, and I need to keep plugging away on Audra's finances."

She'd taken only a couple of steps toward the opening in the fence when Spencer's quiet voice sounded behind her. "It'll work out, Lindsey. Have faith."

A twinge of annoyance rippled up her spine. "Guess Samuel isn't the only 'preacher' in your family."

At his hurt look, she instantly regretted her words.

She swallowed and tried a more tactful tone. "Sorry, but I'm running a bit low in the faith department lately. Afraid I'm stuck with determination and hard work."

When she reached her front porch a few minutes later, she cast a rueful glance toward the Navarro ranch. Good—Spencer was nowhere in sight. He'd been nothing but kind, but she'd had to snap at him. Must be the cumulative stress of quitting her job, worrying over

Audra's state of affairs and wondering what her own future held.

As she started inside, her phone buzzed in her pocket. Retrieving it, she found a text message from Holly Elliot, one of her two best friends from high school. How's it going? Stir-crazy yet?

Lindsey started to text back, then decided she'd much rather hear her friend's voice. She pressed the call icon instead.

"Hey, you!" came Holly's cheery greeting. "Thought you might be too busy to talk."

"Always have time for you." Lindsey detoured to the swing at the far end of the porch and plopped down. "What are you up to?"

"Taking a break while my quiches are in the oven. I'm doing lunch for a ladies' circle at my church." Holly, a widowed single mom, ran a catering service out of her home in Waxahachie. Lindsey pictured her with flour on her nose and her ash-brown curls tucked into a messy bun. "The gig doesn't pay much, but every little bit helps, and anyway, I couldn't turn down this bunch of sweet senior citizens." She lowered her voice. "I'll have to take Davey with me, though. He had a seizure at school yesterday and isn't a hundred percent yet."

"I'm so sorry. Poor little guy." Holly's nine-year-old son had been diagnosed with epilepsy two years ago.

"Oh, but he's a trouper. Says he's happy to help me serve the 'grandmas.' They're always so nice to him at church." The *ding* of a kitchen timer sounded through the phone. "Oops, quiches are done. Can I call you later?"

"Sure. Can't wait to catch up."

As they said goodbye, the wheels in Lindsey's brain began whirring once again. With a little—okay, a *lot*—

of TLC, the chapel and grounds could be turned into a charming site for a country wedding. Her best friend was a culinary school graduate. Lindsey had the business and financial expertise. Now, if only a few more pieces would fall into place, such as several thousand dollars literally dropping from the sky…

Have faith.

"Sorry, Spencer," she muttered on her way inside. If only faith were enough.

She tried, she really did. Even managed a few "Help me!" prayers when things got desperate. But the loving "Daddy-God" her Christian friends spoke of seemed like a myth, or wishful thinking at best. Fathers—human or heavenly—couldn't be counted on. That much, Lindsey knew from experience.

Chapter Three

Another three days went by without Spencer seeing Lindsey again, and every time he paused in his work to look beyond the fence toward the McClement house, his disappointment grew. Yes, drawing upon her financial know-how might help him rescue more horses. But his wanting to talk to her again wasn't only because he'd had to dig deep into his personal bank account to pay Cinnamon's vet bill. Truth be told, until Lindsey had arrived at Audra's last week, he hadn't realized how much he'd missed her all these years.

Exiting the barn, he heard the rumble of the mail truck. Sounded like Lyle the postman had stopped at the McClement box. Since Lindsey's arrival, Spencer had backed off from fetching Audra's mail. If he hurried, though, he could say he just wanted to ask how things were going over there.

As he tucked Audra's mail under his arm and started up the lane, he noticed Lindsey sauntering his way.

She looked up with surprise. "You didn't have to do that. I was just coming down."

"No problem." He handed her the stack of envelopes

along with several ads and Christmas shopping catalogs. "Figured you were staying pretty busy, so I thought I'd ask if y'all needed anything."

"Do we *need* anything?" As she flipped distractedly through the catalogs, her pained expression only deepened. "Nothing discovering a gold mine in the backyard couldn't fix." She glanced toward the house. "Things are even worse than I first thought. You wouldn't believe the credit card debt Audra's racked up just trying to stay afloat. Plus, she owes back taxes on the property, and the county's threatening a foreclosure sale."

Grimacing, Spencer massaged the back of his neck. His concerns seemed trivial next to hers. "I had no idea it'd gotten that bad."

"If only she'd said something months ago—at the funeral, or even last year when Uncle Charles first got so sick—I'd have been here in a flash. Now…" Her shoulders heaved in an exaggerated shrug, and she looked on the verge of tears. "I'm trying my best to keep a whole bunch of smoldering brush fires from turning into one big, blazing inferno."

Spencer ached to help somehow or even say something the least bit encouraging. But only this morning, he'd overheard Dad and Tito discussing the McClement property again, almost as if they anticipated being able to grab it at auction. Wouldn't it be better for Audra in the long run if she set her own price, cut her losses and got out from under this burden? As financially savvy as Lindsey was, surely she'd eventually see the sense in that.

Today, though, it wasn't the smart, capable Lindsey standing before him. Instead, he saw a woman confronted by her own vulnerability, not so different from the twelve-year-old girl who'd cried on his shoulder the summer her parents split up, and it was tearing him up inside. He started to reach for her hand, then pulled back and stuffed his fingers into his jeans pockets. "You'll figure it out, Linds. You always do."

If she'd noticed his clumsy almost-gesture of concern, she didn't show it. Sniffing, she squared her shoulders. "I will. I have no choice. This is the McClement ranch, and I'll do whatever it takes to make sure it stays in the family."

Seemed like she was trying to convince herself, but Spencer saw the doubt in her eyes. "Like I said, if you need anything…" *Soooo* helpful. Frustrated with his powerlessness to fix this for her, he turned to go.

"Thanks for getting the mail," she called after him. "Sorry to be such a downer."

He paused to stare at his boot toes for a moment, then swiveled to face her. "You have nothing to apologize for. And I mean it. Whatever happens, Audra's future couldn't be in better hands."

"Thanks. That means a lot." A smile returning, she tilted her head. "I could be wrong, but when I first saw you walking up the lane, I got the sense you had something else on your mind."

"Not important. I know you're busy—"

"Spencer, spit it out," she said with a crooked grin. Before he could form a response, her brows shot up. "Of course! You said something the other day about needing advice to fund your horse rescue work. I'm so sorry. I've been totally consumed with Audra's affairs—"

"It's okay. Knowing what you're going through, I feel bad for even mentioning it."

"No, don't. Why don't you come inside and we can talk right now?"

He slanted a brow. "If you're sure…"

"Absolutely. Audra has some homemade apple cider in the Crock-Pot. And I can tell you from experience that a steaming mug stirred with a cinnamon stick takes the edge off dealing with money problems."

"All right, then. Thanks." His chest hummed with anticipation that had nothing to do with the apple cider—or Lindsey's offer of advice.

It had everything to do with the chance to spend more time with her.

A few minutes later, they sat at Audra's kitchen table, the tangy-sweet aroma of apple cider wafting from two ceramic mugs. Audra set a plate of molasses cookies between them, then patted Spencer on the shoulder. "My mother's recipe. Lindsey's dad and I used to polish them off faster than she could refill the cookie jar."

Spencer sampled one, the dark, delicious treat practically melting in his mouth. Savoring the sweetness, he nodded his approval. "Even better than your pumpkin bread, and I had to fight off both my parents to claim the last slice."

Audra beamed as if the compliment had made her day. "Help yourself to all you want, and there's more cider, too. I'll be in the living room if y'all need anything else."

"We'll be fine," Lindsey reassured. "You were out at the crack of dawn doing barn chores, then bustling around the kitchen all morning. Go take it easy for a while."

As Audra's footsteps faded, Spencer cast Lindsey a concerned frown. "She looks thinner every time I see her."

"I know. It's all the worry and stress. She cooks like she's feeding an army and then hardly eats a bite." Lindsey rose to fetch a pen and legal pad from the built-in desk. "Okay, let's talk about your money questions."

Her directness caught him off guard. "Afraid I don't even know what questions to ask."

Laughing softly, she shook her head. "Oh, Spencer, you've always had such a big heart. But your knack for strategic planning? Not so great."

He could easily have taken offense, but she was right. When they used to play Mastermind or Battleship as kids, he'd never been able to beat either his brother or Lindsey. After a round or two, he usually gave up and went outside to talk to the horses. "All right, I'm listening. Where do I start?"

"You mentioned forming a nonprofit, which requires some paperwork, including filing for tax-exempt status with the state comptroller. I'm sure I could prevail upon Audra's attorney to help you with that. Unless you have your own, of course."

Glancing in the direction of the Navarro ranch, he frowned. "Probably better if I keep my dealings separate from my dad's."

"Right." Lindsey gave a brisk nod. "Once your nonprofit is established, you'll be able to solicit donations and even recruit volunteers if you need extra help. Be aware, though, you'll have to maintain meticulous records to keep the government entities happy. Are you ready for that kind of commitment?"

"I'm committed to saving horses, so I'm willing to learn." With a little less confidence, he added, "But I'll need a good teacher."

"Don't worry, I'm right here," she said with a light laugh. "We'll take this one step at a time."

With her laptop open to an information page on the Texas Secretary of State website, Lindsey walked him through what establishing a nonprofit entailed. Though most of it was over his head, he could see that the advantages outweighed any reservations he clung to. Then she suggested various ways he could get the word out about his operation and encourage commitments from donors.

When she brought up the idea of creating a website and blog, his eyes glazed over. "Computers and I aren't exactly on speaking terms, Linds. Besides, if I'm hunting and pecking at a keyboard, I'm not out there taking care of the horses. Not to mention my father will be even more annoyed that I'm not doing my part with the family business."

"Then you'll need a staff—people to do the office-type work while you handle the horses." She scribbled on her legal pad again.

"A staff? You've got to be kidding." Had she missed when he'd said he needed to *bring in* more money, not find ways to spend what he didn't have?

"No, I'm not kidding, Spencer. I'm not talking about full-time employees. You'd start by recruiting a volunteer or two. I could even help you out for a few hours a week until your website generates more interest."

Now she was making plans for a website he didn't have for the nonprofit organization he had yet to form. He pushed back his chair, snatched his mug and stalked to the counter.

Lindsey sidled up beside him and rinsed her mug in the sink. "I've overwhelmed you, haven't I?"

"That's a nice way of putting it." More like his head

was about to explode in a massive mushroom cloud. "I appreciate all your suggestions, but…maybe my dad's right and I need to quit dividing my time between the quarter horses and fostering rescues."

"Your dad." Lindsey gave her head a disgusted shake. "Your grandfather, too. Have you ever considered following your own dreams instead of toeing the Navarro line? Isn't that what Samuel did?"

At the mention of his brother, Spencer stiffened. "Samuel may be my twin, but we couldn't be more different."

"Oh, don't I know," she murmured in a tone that snagged something deep in Spencer's heart. "But if you give up now, think of all the starving or mistreated horses you'd have to turn away. Could you live with yourself?"

He couldn't, and that was a huge problem. His chin sank toward his chest.

"I can help you, Spencer." She rested her hand on his forearm. "Trust me."

He wanted to, he really did. "But what about your aunt? Shouldn't you be —"

"Excuse me?" Audra's voice rang out behind him. "Didn't mean to eavesdrop, but sounds carry in an old house. And don't use me as a reason to turn down Lindsey's advice. If my brilliant niece can wrestle bankers and tax men and insurance companies into submission, helping you fund your horse rescue will be a piece of cake."

Glancing at the gloating Lindsey, Spencer couldn't help laughing. "I have no doubt."

"Hey, I know how to blog," Audra announced with a grin, "so I can be your first volunteer. Or second, since Lindsey's technically the first." She moved closer, a pleading smile creasing her lips. "Let me do this, Spencer. I need to feel needed again, and Lindsey says if I don't stop baking, she'll have to go keto or join a gym."

Lindsey heaved a dramatic sigh. "And believe me, giving up carbs is the *last* thing I want to do!"

Cornered by two determined women? He didn't stand a chance. "Okay, yes, thank you. I appreciate the help. But you have to promise to tell me if there's anything at all I can do for you—odd jobs, barn chores, whatever."

After casting her aunt a questioning look and getting a nod in reply, Lindsey stuck out her hand. "You have a deal."

Why did he get the sense there was so much more lurking behind her self-satisfied smile? And why did he feel so guilty for agreeing to this deal when more than likely her efforts to save the ranch would be in vain?

Lindsey wasn't sure yet about the details, but she definitely planned to hold Spencer to their agreement, because if she had any hopes of keeping the McClement ranch in the family, she'd need all the help she could get.

"I'll check with Audra's attorney to make sure we're doing everything right to set up your nonprofit," she said as she followed Spencer to the back door. "In the meantime, I don't want you losing sleep over creating a website. I have a friend who loves doing that kind of thing."

Pausing to glance back, he skewed his jaw. "I can't pay a website designer."

"No worries. It's kind of a hobby for Joella. She'll have fun playing around with ideas and building you a landing page." She spun around to grab the legal pad off the table and wrote her email address, then tore it off and handed it to Spencer. "When you've decided on a name for your nonprofit, drop me a note. And do you have photos of any of your rescues?"

"Yeah, I document each one."

"Perfect. Email me several of your best pictures, especially any before-and-after shots. Joella can use them on the website."

Tucking the paper into his vest pocket, he nodded. "Thanks, Lindsey. I mean it."

"My pleasure." Considering their history, she was more than a little amazed to find herself still so attracted to him. She could stand here all day savoring the entrancing half smile peeking out from beneath his ebony mustache.

He didn't give her the chance. Saying he'd better get back to work, he retreated down the porch steps and started across the backyard.

Too bad his only interest was her brains and business sense. Not that she had time for anything beyond friendship at the moment, or for the foreseeable future. The day was more than half gone, and she still needed to pull together the necessary information for her meeting with Audra's banker first thing tomorrow. Nearly a dozen phone calls this morning had secured extensions from most of Audra's creditors. Now Lindsey hoped to arrange a debt consolidation loan—a start, yes, but only a short-term reprieve and unlikely to help much toward paying off the ranch's back taxes.

With a ragged sigh, she steeled herself to return to Uncle Charles's study. Last week, when she'd first pulled up a chair behind the broad oak desk, it almost felt like trespassing. She'd never forget the many times as a child she'd peeked in to ask her uncle one thing or another, or just to hang out, and he'd pause his work to smile across the desk from his wheelchair. Uncle Charles had been more of a father to her than her real father ever had.

Seated at the desk, she picked up the most recent notice from the county, this one stating a tax sale would be held on March 1 unless property taxes were paid in full before then. How would she ever pull together that much money in less than three months? Memories of Uncle Charles, bitterness toward her absent father, her mounting fear of forfeiting the McClement ranching legacy to a perfect stranger—the weight of it all threatened to smother her.

In a sudden burst of anger, she yanked her cell phone from her pocket. Her father held half ownership in the ranch, and whether he cared to claim it or not, how dare he ignore his sister's struggles? Scrolling through her contacts, she found the seldom-used number and pressed the call icon.

She'd almost convinced herself not to go through with the call when he answered. "Lindsey? Is that you?"

"Hello, Dad." Her throat ached with the effort it took to speak those two words. But now that she had him on the line, she may as well continue. "I'm at Audra's."

Silence. Then, "How is she?"

"If you'd bothered to come to your brother-in-law's funeral, you might have a clue."

"I thought about it. I wanted to. But I was…busy that weekend." Code for *Being with my girlfriend was more important—and besides, you know your mother and I can't occupy the same space.*

Lindsey waved a hand. "Water under the bridge at

this point. I thought you should know the ranch is in trouble. Audra could really use your help."

He huffed a harsh breath. "Linds, I—"

"I don't expect you to show up and start herding cattle or hauling hay." She massaged her forehead. This call was a mistake. "You know what? Forget I said anything." She clicked off.

Audra appeared in the doorway. "You called your dad, didn't you?" Her lips settled into an apologetic frown. "Oh, honey, I should have told you. I've already talked to him."

"You have? When?"

"It was the day before you arrived. I'd gotten a call from someone representing a private corporation interested in buying me out. I owed it to your father to at least make him aware."

Lindsey wasn't sure which upset her more—that Audra had failed to mention the potential buyer or that she'd gone straight to Lindsey's do-nothing dad with the offer. "I don't even have to guess what his reaction was." She clenched her fist around the pencil she'd been holding. "What I don't understand is why you waited so long to tell me."

Her gaze pleading, Audra sank into the nearest chair. "Because I wanted to get your honest, unbiased perspective first about whether you thought there was even the slightest chance of keeping the ranch."

"I'm doing everything I can to make sure of it. And *unbiased*? I couldn't possibly be *more* biased!" Tears formed in Lindsey's eyes. "This ranch means everything to me."

"I know it does, and you know I feel the same way. Which is why I told your dad we needed to hold out a little longer before we even consider selling. Besides," Audra went on with a sardonic smile, "the offer was insultingly lowball, a greedy attempt to steal the ranch out from under me."

Anger subsiding, Lindsey released a relieved chuckle. "Not happening on my watch."

"And I love you all the more for caring so much." Inhaling deeply, Audra rose and extended a hand toward Lindsey. "Come on, young lady, enough brooding over the state of my finances for today. A cold front's blowing in overnight, and I can look after the cows better if we move them to one of the near pastures. You can ride Flash."

"Uncle Charles's horse? But I—"

"No buts. The sun won't be up much longer. Grab your boots and jacket."

With no chance for further argument, Lindsey obeyed. In the barn fifteen minutes later, she had Uncle Charles's handsome sixteen-hand sorrel clipped to the cross ties behind Skeeter, Audra's dun mare. Following Audra into the tack room, she muttered, "Hope I remember how to cinch a saddle."

Audra smirked over her shoulder. "After all the summers you spent here as a kid? No worries. Trust your muscle memory."

Her aunt was right. All it took was starting the cinch strap through the ring, and the rest came naturally. She gave Flash a few minutes to get used to the idea of being under saddle again while she slipped on his bridle. With the stirrups adjusted, she tightened the cinch, then walked Flash outside to the old tree stump Audra used as a mounting block.

Her aunt had already mounted and watched as Lindsey

stretched her leg over the tall horse and hauled herself into the saddle. After settling her feet into the stirrups, Lindsey gathered the reins. "Hey, I did it!"

"Lookin' good up there, sweetie. What did I tell you?" With a laugh, Audra led the way past the barn to the first pasture gate.

It felt strange and somehow comforting to be riding Uncle Charles's horse. Lindsey couldn't help missing her grandparents' gentle bay gelding she used to ride as a kid, but Sport was already in his late teens back then, and Audra had written a couple of years ago that he'd suffered a bad bout of colic and she'd had to put him down. Though Flash was as calm as Sport and even smarter, the view from Flash's saddle made the ground seem so much farther away.

After they'd passed through two more gates, they came upon fourteen white-faced Herefords, the last of the McClement herd. Lindsey couldn't keep her thoughts from drifting to happier times when the ranch was thriving. Close to two hundred head of cattle had once roamed the hilly pastures, and Grandpa had been so proud of Old Jack, his prize bull.

Circling Skeeter around behind the herd, Audra whistled and waved her lariat to get the cows moving toward the open gate. Lindsey mainly tried to stay out of the way while keeping an eye out for any cows making a break in the opposite direction.

Then one did and Audra shouted, "Keep 'em moving forward, Linds. I've got to chase down that confounded heifer."

Great. Herding cattle was way outside Lindsey's realm of expertise. At least Flash seemed to know his job, so Lindsey slacked up on the reins and gave him his head. His sharp back-and-forth maneuvers quickly had her clutching the saddle horn and praying she wouldn't get thrown. Would Audra ever get back with the runaway cow?

"Need some help?"

She raised her head to see Spencer riding through the gate. At the same moment, Flash jigged to the left and her boot slipped out of the stirrup. Just as she felt herself sliding off on the right, Spencer rode up beside her, steadying her with a grip on her elbow.

Once she'd regained her seat, he released her arm. "You okay?"

"Yeah, thanks." She whooshed out a breath, relieved to see the bawling cows were closing ranks and making their way toward the next pasture. With Flash back under her control, she gave her full attention to Spencer. "What are you doing here?"

"Heard the weather report about the time I saw you and Audra ride out. Figured you were bringing in the herd and wanted to make sure you managed okay."

"We're managing just fine." Lindsey gave an embarrassed grin. "Can't you tell?"

Just then, the feisty red heifer trotted past and nosed in at the rear of the herd pushing through the gate. Audra reined Skeeter to a halt on Lindsey's other side. "Good work, Linds. Hi, Spencer. Nice of you to lend a hand."

He tipped his hat. "Didn't do a thing."

Except ride up like my knight in shining armor to keep me from landing on my rear. Attention fixed on the cows, Lindsey clucked to her horse. "Better get 'em through and close the gate before they change their minds."

* * *

Spunky and independent as ever. Spencer adjusted his Stetson, then took up drag position as Lindsey and Audra drove the herd through the next pasture and into a smaller one behind the barn. After closing the last gate, he rode alongside Audra. "Anything else I can do to help?"

"We can take it from here, but thank you." The woman offered a quick smile, her attention on the lowing cattle. "Lindsey, go on to the barn with Flash. I'll be along soon as I fill the water trough and toss out some hay for these girls."

Spencer exchanged a look with Lindsey, her pursed lips communicating their shared misgivings about leaving Audra to finish on her own. He turned back toward Audra. "I can sling hay for you. Those bales can get pretty heavy."

She'd already dismounted and was securing her horse to the fence rail. Shoulders stiffening, she turned. "You're a gentleman to offer, but if I can't manage my cattle by myself, then what's the point—" Her lips trembled, and she covered her mouth with her hand.

Lindsey swung down from her horse and ran to her aunt's side. "It's going to be all right," she murmured, drawing Audra into a hug. "Nobody expects you to do this alone. That's why I'm here, isn't it?"

While Lindsey comforted her aunt, Spencer gathered Flash's reins. The least he could do was take care of their horses for them. Leaving Annie, his bay mare, tied to a hitching post outside the barn, he led the late Charles Forrester's big sorrel inside and clipped him between the cross ties. As he removed the saddle, he noticed a faint freeze brand partially hidden beneath the horse's mane—a circle surrounding a script *N*.

The Navarro brand.

So at some point since the feud began, the two families had done business together. Otherwise, how could Charles have owned and ridden a Navarro-registered quarter horse? Spencer hoped for an opportunity to bring it up later with his father, preferably when Tito was otherwise occupied.

By the time he returned to the pasture for Audra's horse, she and Lindsey had scattered several flakes of fresh hay for the cattle. The lazy animals munched idly, as if they couldn't care less about the predicted arctic blast.

Audra separated out a couple more flakes, then straightened and dusted off her hands. She was breathing hard, but an air of confidence had returned. "That should do it, Lindsey. They'll be fine till morning."

Spencer slipped through the gate. "Flash is in his stall. I put away his tack and gave him fresh water."

"Oh, Spencer." Audra looked surprised he was still there. "You didn't have to do that—"

"But thank you," Lindsey interrupted with a chiding glance toward her aunt. To Audra, she said, "The wind's picking up. Why don't you go on to the house and get warm. I'll take care of Skeeter."

"But I still need to feed the horses and put out food and water for the barn cats."

"I know the drill by now. Please." Holding open the gate, Lindsey firmly waved her aunt through.

Spencer untied Skeeter from the fence, then fell into step beside Lindsey. Once Audra was safely out of earshot, he murmured, "Not sure which of you is more stubborn. Audra shouldn't even be trying to run this place by herself."

Lindsey spun on him. "I fully realize this is too big a job for one person. But once we're operating in the black again—and we will be—I intend to stay on until we've hired some reliable help for my aunt going forward."

About time Spencer learned when to keep his mouth shut. Because as much as he valued her expertise concerning funding for his rescue horses, when it came to accepting ranch management advice, Lindsey didn't reciprocate.

Chapter Four

Arms locked across her abdomen, Audra stood in the doorway of Charles's study. "How's it looking? Any more hopeful?"

"Too soon to say." Lindsey tore her gaze from the computer screen, where she'd been poring over figures since their exhausting meeting at the bank that morning. She'd been able to wrangle a consolidation loan for Audra's credit card debt but only after she'd agreed to cosign. She'd done so willingly, of course, even with the understanding that she'd committed to being the responsible party should Audra fail to make repayment.

Yes, she had a fair amount put aside in savings, but if her unemployed status continued, the money wouldn't last indefinitely. Aunt Audra's prayer that Lindsey would find a suitable job with a decent salary in small-town Gabriel Bend simply wasn't realistic.

"Sorry I can't be more help." Sighing, Audra came around and perched on the edge of the desk next to Lindsey. "I'll never be able to thank you enough for all you're doing. And Spencer," she went on, regret shading her tone. "I was so ungracious to him yesterday, when he was only being neighborly."

"I'm sure he understands." Although Lindsey wasn't sure *she* did. His repeated hints about selling the ranch were getting under her skin…perhaps because the almost constant knot in her belly suggested he might be right?

Hands clasped, Audra stared at the floor. "Whatever happens, honey, I don't want you blaming yourself. Because even if we do lose the ranch, it wouldn't be the end of the world. It's just a house and a few cows and a chunk of land. What matters most is—" Eyes brimming, she forced out her next word on a shaky breath. "Family."

Lindsey appreciated what her aunt was saying. A part of her even believed it. Even so, it took effort to keep from snapping back with a few thoughts of her own about *family*. The concept had clearly been lost on her father. Keeping her tone level, she stated, "I care about family, too. Which is why the McClement ranch is going to *stay* the McClement ranch, whatever it takes."

Audra cast her a sad but knowing smile. "This is still about your dad, isn't it?"

Teeth clenched, Lindsey looked away. "He should never have turned his back on his inheritance." *He should never have abandoned Mom and me!*

"You have to let it go, sweetie." Bending to envelop Lindsey in a hug, Audra gave her a tender squeeze. "Hanging on to bitterness only hurts you. It isn't going to change your father."

Lindsey released a sharp sigh and wrapped her arms around her aunt's gaunt frame. Cheek pressed against Audra's soft flannel shirt, she caught the faint smell of wood smoke from the living room's potbelly stove. "But it's so unfair," she muttered. "Dad's only interest in the ranch now is what he can get out of it if you sell."

"Which won't be much if that corporate offer is the best we can expect." Straightening, Audra harrumphed. "How about we get our minds on a cheerier topic? Christmas is just around the corner. Think your mom and Stan would fly out for a few days so we can all spend the holidays together?"

Thankful her mother had found happiness when she'd remarried and moved to Florida a few years ago, Lindsey smiled. "That would be nice. I'll call later and ask."

"We'll need to get busy baking and decorating." Audra tapped her chin as she moved toward the door. "I'll start making lists."

If only Lindsey could distract herself so easily. "I'll come help in a few minutes." With an inner groan, she returned her attention to the accounting program on Charles's desktop computer.

Her laptop, also open on the desk, chimed to announce an incoming email. Reading Spencer's name in the sender's line, she hesitated to open the message. But the subject line read, *Sorry. Forgive me?* So how could she resist?

I overstepped yesterday. Whatever you and Audra decide to do with the ranch is your business, not mine. If there's ever anything I can do, though, the offer still stands. In the meantime, you asked for some photos. Sending a few you might like. BTW, how does New Start Equine Rescue sound for a name?

Short and sweet—typical Spencer. She couldn't help smiling as she began scrolling through the pictures.

Moments later, she found her eyes tearing up at the incredible transformations the photos portrayed. From skin-and-bones and drooping heads to bright eyes and healthy musculature, each set of pictures told the story of Spencer's loving attention. His skill as a horseman was undeniable, and no matter how things turned out for the McClement ranch or where life took her after her work here was done, Lindsey promised herself she'd do everything in her power to help Spencer launch his rescue program.

She'd start right now by giving her friend Joella James a call. With Audra puttering around in the kitchen again, Lindsey padded over to nudge the door partway closed, then took out her cell phone and plopped into the desk chair.

She caught the sophisticated blonde businesswoman in the middle of haggling with a hotel manager over the too-small room he'd reserved for a huge corporate awards banquet. "It's okay, Joella. You can call me later when you have more time."

"No, please." Her friend's voice dropped to barely above a whisper. "You're saving me from chewing this jerk's head off!" Joella excused herself to the manager with over-the-top politeness, then adjusted her voice to a normal tone. "Of course, Ms. McClement. How can I help you?"

"Smooth. Very smooth." Lindsey snickered. "Glad I could be of assistance. Now…perhaps I could twist your arm to do a favor for me?"

"If I can, sure. What's up?"

Lindsey described what she wanted to do for Spencer.

"He wouldn't need anything fancy, just a basic site with photos highlighting his equine rescue program along with a link for registering as a donor or volunteer."

"Hold on here." Joella's tone turned disbelieving. "Is this the same Spencer Navarro who dissed you in front of all of Gabriel Bend?"

"We were kids, and he apologized." She put a hand to her forehead. "Don't make a big deal about this. Besides the fact that he's amazing with horses, he's been really kind to Audra this past year. I'm just returning the favor."

"Mmm-hmm. You still have a crush on him, don't you?"

"I do *not*." And whom was she trying to convince? "Can I enlist your web design skills or not?"

Joella sighed. "Email me some details and I'll put together a rough draft."

"Thank you so much, Jo-Jo. I won't keep you, then—"

"No hurry. The crabby manager can cool his heels a bit longer. Besides, we haven't had a good long talk in ages. How's it going with your aunt's affairs?"

Lindsey gave her a condensed version of the last few days. "So I'm scrounging for ways to get her out of debt without losing the ranch."

"Tough. I know what the place means to you."

Lindsey rose and paced in front of the windows. Beyond the barn, the cows they'd brought in yesterday afternoon grazed on hay and winter grass. "Since I've been here, an idea has started percolating." She chewed her lip. "But I'm afraid it's way more ambitious than I should even be considering."

Joella harrumphed. "Am I talking to the same person who insisted we could replicate the ballroom from

Beauty and the Beast in a big, bare convention hall for our high school prom? When did you ever shy away from an ambitious project?"

"Prom was eleven years ago. College and the corporate world have been a major reality check."

"Tell me about it. Being an event planner was always my dream, but…lately it's been more stressful than I signed up for. Besides, I'm sick of these big-company execs who think all it takes to get their way is to shell out more cash. They don't seem to understand there are limits to what money can buy."

A gust of icy wind shook the windowpanes and forced its way between the sill and frame. Caulking and weather stripping—more repairs for the constantly growing to-do list. "If they wanted to toss some cash my aunt's way, neither of us would complain."

"I'll make a note," Joella said with a dry laugh. "So tell me your idea. I love doling out unsolicited opinions."

Lindsey tiptoed into the hallway to peek in on Audra. Surrounded by measuring cups, cracked eggshells and the flour canister, she had the mixer running again. Just what Lindsey needed—more cookies. She returned to the study. "It's the ranch. It's so beautiful here—or at least it was in its heyday."

"What are you getting at, Linds?" Joella's tone had softened.

"I'm not completely sure yet, but I keep thinking there should be a way to monetize this place. A way to keep it in the family and generate some income until things stabilize enough for my aunt to get back to the business of cattle ranching."

"Like a bed-and-breakfast or something?"

"A B and B may be *too* ambitious, at least for now. I'm thinking about some kind of outdoor event venue, like for weddings and such. You've visited here with me in the spring and summer a few times, remember?"

"How could I forget? And that cute little storage building that used to be a chapel—surrounded by trees and flowers in bloom, the place was a photographer's dream."

"I think it could be again." Lindsey sighed inwardly as her gaze swept the barren backyard. "But you have to spend money to make money, and that's my current sticking point. When I'm hoarding every penny to pay the back taxes, there's nothing left to spend on other things."

A soft exhalation preceded Joella's thoughtful silence. "How does your aunt feel about this plan?"

"It's nowhere near a 'plan' yet, and I haven't even mentioned it to Audra."

"But if this could be a way for her to keep the ranch *and* pay the bills…what's keeping you from at least giving it a try?"

"You really think I should?"

"What are you risking besides a little time if you create a preliminary business plan and approach a few possible investors?"

"We could start small, do it in stages." Lindsey's pulse quickened as the idea took hold. "Maybe pitch the location to photographers while we work toward developing the grounds as a wedding venue. I talked to Holly the other day and was thinking how great it would be if she'd move to Gabriel Bend and become our caterer."

"I think you're onto something, Linds. Holly and Davey would love it there. And if only I could leave be-

hind big-city Dallas and corporate event planning..."
Joella sighed. "I'd give anything to move down there
and help you make this happen."

"Oh, Jo-Jo, nothing would make me happier."

"Of course, I'd expect you to reintroduce me to Spencer's amazingly good-looking brother the next time he's
in town."

Lindsey smirked. "They're identical twins, you know."

"I do. So why are you still on the phone with me
when your handsome horse rescuer is next door?"

"I'm going to pretend you didn't say that." Lindsey
dropped into the desk chair. "Go straighten things out
with your horsey hotel manager. I have a bunch more
of Audra's financial records to dig through yet today."

"Don't give up on your idea, though, Linds. You
can do this."

"Thanks for the vote of confidence. And thanks for
saying yes to building Spencer a website. I'll email you
more details shortly."

Round-penning one of the quarter horse yearlings,
Spencer shook his head. Moments before he'd hit Send
on his email to Lindsey, he'd suffered serious second
thoughts. For one thing, she had plenty already on her
plate. For another, between the learning curve and the
time commitment, could he realistically handle everything entailed in operating a nonprofit equine rescue?
And maintaining a website—Lindsey must not have a
clue how computer illiterate he was. He'd had to break
down and ask his mom how to attach photos to a message.

After returning the yearling to the pasture, he saddled another of the horses for a training ride in the
arena. The speedy little mare was almost ready for her

new owner, Jenny Thomas, an up-and-coming barrel racer willing to pay top dollar for her next mount in hopes of winning big rodeo purses. Breathing almost as hard as the mare, he completed the cloverleaf pattern and galloped across an invisible finish line. No doubt this horse would quickly prove her worth.

"She looks good," his father called from the end of the arena. "A little wide around the second barrel, but you've done well with her."

A rare compliment Spencer would gratefully accept. "She's built for barrel racing. Calm and focused at the start, plenty of power in the hindquarters for those turns." He swung to the ground and walked the horse over to the fence rail. "I'd like to give her two more weeks of training, then have Jenny come over and try her out."

"Good plan." Spencer's father opened the gate for him. "Did you fix the leak in the yearling barn watering system like I asked?"

"All done."

"And the latch on Concho's stall?"

"Changed it out for something a little more challenging." Their prize breeding stallion had recently figured out how to open his gate and go exploring.

With a crisp nod, his father adjusted his Stetson and marched off. Not so much as a thank-you, naturally. Spencer had grown up with the man's brusque manner, but sometimes it still stung—and only made him more determined to prove himself by making his equine rescue efforts self-sustaining. Dad had great love and respect for horses, so his attitude had nothing to do with the nature of Spencer's undertaking.

No, Hank Navarro simply couldn't stomach the idea

of losing both his sons' full commitment to the family business.

With the mare untacked and settled into her stall for the night, Spencer strode over to the small barn to check on Cinnamon, then went to the house to clean up before supper.

His mother, stirring something on the stove, greeted him with an air-kiss. She wrinkled her nose. "You smell like horse."

Tossing his Stetson onto the hat rack, he snorted. "If you aren't used to horse smells by now—"

"Just an observation, *mijo*. I'm quite fond of *aroma de caballo*." Lois Navarro might not be Latina, but after thirty-six years as Hank's wife and Arturo's daughter-in-law, she'd picked up enough Spanish to hold her own. Smiling, she tilted her head. "Can't help but notice you've been spending a lot more time next door. Nice to have Lindsey around again, isn't it?"

How was he supposed to answer that without putting ideas into his mother's head? She'd always favored Lindsey, never letting the Navarro-McClement feud get in the way. "She's giving me advice about starting an equine rescue nonprofit. She even has a friend who can build me a website."

"Wow, you're going all out with this venture. And my son getting all techy with a website—never thought I'd see the day."

"And you haven't seen it yet." Good thing Dad and Tito hadn't come in yet. He'd just as soon leave them out of the loop until his plans solidified.

His mother sampled a spoonful from the simmering pot, then added a pinch of something from the spice rack. "Well, I'm proud of you for taking the initiative."

"Thanks, Mom." Whatever she was cooking smelled a million times better than Spencer's clothes. Tweaking her more-salt-than-pepper braid with one hand, he reached around with the other to snatch her spoon and steal a taste for himself. "Mmm, Lita's chili recipe." His late grandmother had made the best. "Needs more cilantro."

"Now you fancy yourself a chef? Better stick to horses, young man. And please, go get cleaned up."

He started toward the hall, then backtracked. The question about Charles Forrester's horse had been nagging at him, and maybe his mother could fill in the blanks. "Hey, Mom, yesterday while I was helping put Audra's horses in the barn, I noticed Flash's brand."

A knowing smile creased her lips. "The Navarro *N*. Yes, Flash was one of ours."

"But how? When?"

With a quick glance toward the back door, his mother turned down the stove burner and swiveled to face him. "After Charles was wounded in Iraq, he went through several months of rehab, including a therapeutic riding program. Audra confided in me once that for weeks after he'd come home, she'd been terrified of losing him to the depths of depression. But after he was on horseback again—the freedom, the empowerment—he started coming back to life."

Spencer gave a low whistle. "That's pretty amazing."

"Around the same time, I'd heard your grandfather carrying on about a young gelding he'd been trying to train. He claimed the horse lacked the Navarro spirit and would never be good for anything except some kid's backyard pleasure horse."

"I sort of remember that. Didn't Dad and Tito argue about putting the horse down?"

His mother offered a grim nod as she gave the chili another stir. "Arturo is a *charro* through and through. You've heard the stories of how he grew up watching his father compete in *charreadas*."

The Mexican horsemen and their traditional rodeos. "And then followed in his father's footsteps." It was a great source of pride for Tito. Though Spencer had personally never cared to participate, he respected the ritualized team competition for its roots in ranching and horsemanship skills. "But what does that have to do with Charles Forrester owning Flash?"

"Your dad had recently begun attending natural horsemanship clinics, and he and your grandfather were at odds over old-school versus new-school training methods." As if it had been her own idea, Mom added more fresh cilantro to the chili. "Then one weekend Arturo's *charro* team planned to compete in a *charreada* near San Antonio. He told your father not to waste any more time or Navarro resources on the horse and to get rid of him one way or another by the time he returned."

"So Dad sold him to the Forresters?"

"Not sold. Gave. He had a sense the sweet-tempered horse would be perfect for Charles."

Spencer was momentarily speechless. "And Tito never found out?"

"How would he?" With a roll of her eyes, Mom went to get something from the pantry. "Your grandfather hasn't set foot on McClement land since the day he and Egan legally parted ways."

Just then, someone rapped on the back door. Through the sheer lace curtain, Spencer made out Lindsey's profile. Pulse rate increasing, he hauled in a breath and opened the door. "Lindsey. Hi." He peered past her shoulder in hopes his dad and grandfather hadn't finished yet with the horse they'd been training. Anything to shield Lindsey from Tito's ill will toward the McClements. "Is everything okay?"

"Hanging in there. Audra's been baking again and insisted I bring you some cookies." She handed him a foil-covered paper plate, then leaned past him. "Hi, Mrs. Navarro."

"Lindsey, honey. I've been meaning to pop over and say hello ever since you got to town. How's your aunt doing?"

"She has good days and bad. If I could only get her to eat a full meal…" Lindsey's mouth puckered in a troubled frown.

"Grief takes time, and she's had a harder time than most, even before Charles took sick. Having you here is sure to be a blessing." Spencer's mother beamed a meaningful smile in his direction. "In more ways than one."

Still holding the plate of cookies, Spencer shot his mother a pointed glance before returning his attention to Lindsey. "Hope you got my email. Did the photos come through?"

"They were perfect. Thank you." Urgency darkening her brown eyes, Lindsey lowered her voice. "Do you have a few minutes to talk?"

"Sure." He set the cookies on the counter, then motioned her into the family room and slid the glass-paneled double doors closed—less chance of Tito walking in on them. "What's on your mind?"

"Remember the idea I told you about?"

Guessing where this was headed, he kept his expression neutral. "You mean for turning the ranch into an event venue?"

She fingered a lock of her hair. "I'm starting to think it could actually work, but I'm about to come apart at the seams trying not to say anything in front of my aunt for fear of getting her hopes up."

How about your own? he wanted to ask. "If anyone has the smarts to make it happen, it's you, Lindsey. But…aren't you running out of time?"

"Exactly why we'd need to get started right away. I know what a huge undertaking it would be. But I've talked with a couple of friends—Holly runs a successful catering business, and Joella, who's building your website, is a corporate event planner—and they've made me believe it's doable." She pulled her lower lip between her teeth. "So I guess what I'm asking is, would you be willing to help? I'd figure out a way to pay you somehow…eventually…"

"*Pay* me? No, not after—" Booming voices from the kitchen drew his attention. Dad and Tito must have come in. He hated to imagine his grandfather's reaction if he found out what Lindsey was hoping to do next door. "You should go. We can talk about this later."

Mouth flattened, she looked toward the door, then back at Spencer. "It always comes back to the feud, doesn't it? Want me to climb out a window so your grandfather doesn't see me?"

"No. I'm only trying—"

"What is wrong with the Navarros that you can't let go of this senseless grudge? Arturo's resentment has infected all of you."

"That's not true."

"Isn't it? Maybe not your mother—she's never been anything but kind." Her voice rose with every word. "But the rest of you—"

"Lindsey, please." He stretched one hand toward her.

She backed away, her eyes narrowing in a look that stabbed like an ice shard. "What was I thinking? You said it yourself twelve years ago—*Navarros and Mc-Clements don't mix*."

Chin held high, she shoved the doors apart and marched from the room. Spencer unfroze his feet to follow, only to catch her quick goodbye to his mother as she barged past Dad and Tito and out the back door.

Chapter Five

"Was that the McClement girl?" Jaw clenched beneath his silver mustache, Tito glared at Spencer. "Haven't I told you again and again that you should not be associating with her kind?"

"Her *kind*?" Bile rose in Spencer's throat. "What's that supposed to mean?"

"You know very well. She's the granddaughter of the man who stole everything I had worked for—everything that mattered to me." He jabbed a finger in the direction of the McClement ranch. "That land will be mine in repayment if it is the last thing I do."

Spencer's dad laid a hand on Tito's extended arm. "Papi...not now."

"Why not? Doesn't your son have a right to know of my intentions to reclaim his inheritance?" Casting a haughty smile toward Spencer, the old man narrowed his eyes. "This grandson, at least, has not completely turned his back on his heritage."

Choosing to ignore the veiled reference to his twin, Spencer squared off with his grandfather. "It's true, isn't it—you're looking to buy the McClement ranch out from under Audra Forrester. Don't we have plenty of land already? Why can't you leave her alone, give her a chance to recover and make a go of things?"

"Boys, boys," his mother interrupted in the cajoling tone only she could get away with. "Don't make me send you to your rooms without supper."

"Apologies, *mi amor*." Outside Tito's line of vision, Spencer's father shot him a look that said, *Drop it*. "Come on, Papi. Let's wash up."

Mom handed Spencer a ladle and pointed to the bowls she'd set on the table. "You can dish out the chili."

Grabbing a bowl, he muttered, "How do you put up with him?"

"Because he's your father's father and also because I know beneath all that bitterness is a tender heart that hasn't forgotten how to love."

Spencer would have to ponder that statement awhile longer. He served some chili from the pot on the stove, then took the bowl to the table and brought over another empty one. "What really happened, Mom? All my life, I've felt like I haven't gotten the whole story."

"It began long before I met your dad, of course." She took a pan of corn muffins from the oven and emptied them into a napkin-lined basket. "He was barely five years old when Arturo and Egan had their falling-out. Your aunt Alicia was only two. It's not a subject your grandfather willingly talks about, so all they really know is what little they've pieced together over the years. Apparently, the disagreements had been building for a long time before something happened that severed the friendship forever." Setting the basket on the table, she gave a weary shrug. "Whatever that *something* was, your grandfather hasn't been able to let it go. Then after the ranch was divided, he believed the McClements cheated him out of the best grazing land and water resources."

Just then, Spencer's dad returned to the kitchen. "Lois, what are you telling our son?"

"Only answering his questions as best I can." She looked past him toward the hallway. "Is your father coming to supper?"

"He said he's too upset to eat and was going to bed." Dad rubbed his jaw. "Papi hasn't been looking well lately. I'm going to try to get him in soon to see the doctor."

"Stubborn old coot. I'll believe it when I see it." With an annoyed shake of her head, Mom motioned Spencer and his dad to the table.

While his father offered the blessing, Spencer's mind drifted to remnants of stories he'd heard about the friendship gone sour between Arturo Navarro and Egan McClement. According to one version, Egan had shown no respect for the *charro* traditions of Arturo's Mexican ancestors and refused to diversify into breeding quarter horses. Another rumor suggested there may have been a romantic rivalry, which, having seen firsthand how devoted both men were to their loving wives, Spencer had a hard time believing. In any case, it sounded like they were both too bullheaded to admit fault or to compromise.

But was stubborn pride reason enough for two best friends to so spitefully part ways? For Arturo and Egan, apparently so.

Lindsey should never have trusted Spencer's apology, much less his attempts at friendship. Naturally he'd choose loyalty to his family over any regard for her. It was about time she accepted there'd never be an end to the differences between Navarros and McClements.

She refrained from saying as much to Audra, though, and had no intention of mentioning her blowup with Spencer or the indignant glare the elder Navarro had shot her as she'd hurried past him on her way out. Knowing it would be impossible to keep her emotions under wraps, she called it an early night and went straight upstairs to her room.

The next morning, she awoke to a quiet house and a wintry sun already high on the horizon. Sitting up with a jolt, she mentally scolded herself for sleeping so late and leaving Audra to tackle the early-morning ranch chores alone. After pulling on a flannel shirt, jeans and boots, she tucked her phone into her pocket and jogged down to the kitchen.

Audra was coming through the back door, Spencer right behind her. "Coffee's hot. Help yourself." She slipped out of her coat and gloves, her smile warming when she saw Lindsey. "There's our sleepyhead. Mornin', sweetie. I left you some oatmeal on the stove."

Casting Spencer an uneasy glance, she turned to her aunt. "Why didn't you wake me?"

"You looked so exhausted last night, I didn't have the heart. Anyway, Spencer came over bright and early insisting on lending a hand, so we were done in a jiff." Audra took the carton of half-and-half from the fridge. "Cream, Spencer?" When he declined, she stirred a dollop into her own mug.

Pouring coffee for herself, Lindsey watched Spencer from the corner of her eye. He sipped his brew while standing near the door, as if uncertain whether he should go or stay. *Go* would suit her just fine.

Audra took a bowl from the cupboard and served oatmeal for Lindsey. "Sit down and eat while it's hot. How about some raisins and brown sugar?"

"I can get it myself." Lindsey immediately regretted the sharpness in her tone. Why, oh why, did Spencer have to come over, and why didn't he leave?

"Spencer, hang up your jacket and take a seat. Lindsey won't bite." Audra motioned them to the table. With a meaningful smile, she excused herself and left the kitchen.

Lindsey eased into the chair farthest from Spencer's. "Why are you—"

"About last night—" he said at the same time.

They both grew silent, Spencer staring into his coffee mug and Lindsey poking a spoon into the oatmeal she had no appetite for.

"Lindsey," he began softly, "will you please let me explain?"

"I don't know what else needs to be said." Sighing, she laid down her spoon. "Don't worry, I'll still make sure you get your nonprofit forms filed, and my friend's already working on your website—"

He rapped his clenched fist on the table. "I don't care about any of that right now. I just want *us* to be okay again."

The quiet force behind his words made her blink. There was an *us*?

"I never meant to blow off your ideas last night," he went on. "But I know my grandfather, and when I heard him come in, all I could think about was protecting you. I couldn't put you in the position of having to deal with him."

She hiked a brow. "You're sure it wasn't to spare your grandfather from having to deal with a McClement?"

"Uh, maybe a tiny bit." He cast her a hopeful grin. "So can you forgive me? Again?"

Wow, he was making it hard to stay mad. Not to mention she still couldn't get over the grown-up Spencer's rakish good looks. "Guess I owe you an apology, too. As generous as you've been, doing things for my aunt without even being asked, I had no right to say the things I did."

"So…truce?" Spencer came around the table and offered Lindsey his hand.

She gazed thoughtfully at him. "Enemies make truces. Friends forgive and move on."

"Then I'm all for friendship."

"Me, too." Rising, she took his hand and gave it a solid shake. "If only…"

"Yeah, if only." With a quick breath, he edged toward the door and retrieved his jacket and hat from the coat tree. "I should get home. My dad has a list of jobs waiting for me."

"I'll walk you out." After donning her barn coat, Lindsey snatched her untouched bowl of oatmeal. "Just going to dump this somewhere so Audra doesn't find out I didn't eat my breakfast like a good girl."

They moved onto the porch. "Speaking of which, how's Audra's appetite? Any better?"

"Maybe a little. Getting a consolidation loan approved yesterday eased her mind some." A tremor squeaked up Lindsey's spine. "Kind of unnerving for me as cosigner, but at least it's a start on paying down her debts."

"Sounds like a big step for both of you."

"Tell me about it! When I quit my job to come here, getting this deeply committed wasn't even on my radar." They'd walked to the edge of the yard nearest the barn, and Lindsey paused to empty her bowl behind a scraggly bush. Shouldn't be long before birds or varmints made quick work of it.

"And now you're talking about turning this place into an event venue." Spencer whistled through his teeth. "I mean it, Lindsey. Tell me how I can help."

"Even considering how your grandfather feels about McClements?"

"You shouldn't have to worry about that. I'll deal with any fallout."

His cell phone buzzed. When he checked the display, his jaw tensed. "It's the livestock deputy. I'd better take this." He walked away to answer the call.

From Spencer's side of the conversation, Lindsey gathered the deputy was on his way over with another rescue horse. Spencer said he'd meet the deputy at the ranch in a few minutes.

As he ended the call, Lindsey could sense his distress. "Is it bad?"

"The horse? Not nearly as bad as some. Just hoping my dad won't say no like he's been threatening to." Frowning, he firmed his Stetson lower on his brow and started across the field toward the ugly barbed-wire fence.

Lindsey watched him go, her heart aching that his father would deny him the chance to do something he cared so much about. There might be some logic in Mr. Navarro's concerns about exposing his quarter horses to disease. If only Spencer could stable his rescues at another location, well away from the Navarro horses but close enough that he could come and go easily...

She glanced over her shoulder at Audra's immense barn, now home only to Skeeter, Flash and the occasional cow or calf that might need extra attention.

The sheriff's department SUV and horse trailer had turned in at the Navarros'. Spencer met the deputy as he stepped from the vehicle, and moments later Spencer's father charged over from the arena to intercept them. Though Lindsey couldn't hear what they were saying, she could tell from their gestures that Mr. Navarro didn't want the horse to stay.

On impulse, she took her phone from her pocket and hurriedly typed a text to Spencer. Bring the horse over here. You can use our barn.

She hit Send, then watched for Spencer to check his phone. At first, he seemed too embroiled in arguing with his father to read the message. Then he did a double take, and his gaze sought out Lindsey's across the field. Even from this distance, she made out his questioning stare. She nodded sharply and waved.

More animated discussion followed before Spencer climbed into the deputy's passenger seat and Mr. Navarro threw up his hands and marched off.

Within minutes, the deputy parked his SUV next to Audra's barn, and Lindsey decided she probably should have cleared this with her aunt first.

"Give me a sec," she said as the men opened their doors. "I'll be right back."

Inside, she went looking for Audra and found her in the downstairs master bedroom folding laundry. "Um, Aunt Audra..."

Her aunt narrowed her eyes. "The last time you used

that tone with me, you were fifteen years old and had accidentally left the pasture gate open."

"And I'm still so, so sorry about what the cows did to your vegetable garden." Hands clasped, Lindsey inched closer. "I promise, this isn't nearly as awful, but I did, um, kind of tell Spencer he could use one of your barn stalls for a rescue horse."

Audra clucked her tongue. "Oh, honey, why'd you think I'd mind? Of course he can use our barn. It'll take some effort to get one of the vacant stalls ready, but if we get started now—"

"Actually, they're parked out back and ready to unload."

Waiting for Lindsey to return from the house, Spencer struggled with competing emotions. On the one hand, he couldn't be more thankful that God had brought Lindsey back into his life, and not only because of everything she was doing so that he could save more horses.

However, her return to Gabriel Bend was creating all kinds of problems for Spencer within his own family. In addition to Tito's ongoing animosity toward the McClements, Dad had made his opinion perfectly clear concerning Spencer's stabling his rescues in Audra's barn. Did any hope remain that God would someday heal the rift between the Navarros and McClements? The only answer was to keep praying.

Deputy Miller had entered the barn to take a look around. He came out rubbing his chin. "Don't know if I can okay this, Spencer. The stalls where Mrs. Forrester keeps her animals are the only ones in decent shape. There's a hole in the roof over the stalls at the back, and several of the gates are busted or hanging on rusty hinges. A lot of work needs to be done before I'd declare it safe for fostering rescues."

"I'll be lending a hand with repairs around here anyway. I'll put those items at the top of my list." Spencer strode over to a sheltered paddock attached to the barn. "The weather's supposed to be milder through next weekend. The horse could stay outside for a day or two while I fix the roof and get a barn stall cleaned up and ready. That'll also give the vet time to check him out before I move him into the barn with Audra's horses."

"That could work. You'd blanket him at night?"

"Of course. And check on him throughout the day."

A moment later, Lindsey and Audra stepped out to the porch. "Good morning, Deputy," Audra called. She walked over to shake the officer's hand. "Spencer's more than welcome to use our barn and pasture for his rescue horses. I know things aren't in the best of shape right now, but we intend to work on that."

While Audra and Deputy Miller talked more about the necessary releases and boarding arrangements, Spencer sidled over to Lindsey. "Can't thank you enough for this."

"Will you be able to smooth things over with your dad?"

He shrugged. "As long as I don't shirk my duties with our own horses, I think he'll come around."

Something else nagged at him, though. If, despite Lindsey's best efforts, Audra was forced to sell and Tito bought the McClement ranch like he hoped, Audra's house, barn and pastures would all become Navarro property. In that case, Spencer could easily run his equine rescue operation separate from the Navarro quarter horses while also keeping everything in the family.

And he'd likely never see Lindsey again.

He found her studying him. "Still worried about your dad's reaction?"

Before he was forced to come up with at least a partially honest reply, Deputy Miller joined them. "Ready to get the horse unloaded and into the paddock?"

The aging gray gelding stumbled as the deputy backed him off the trailer. Ribs poking out, head drooping, the animal barely took notice of his surroundings, as if one more stop on the journey to his final end made no difference. By providing the love, care and attention this horse deserved, Spencer hoped he'd have the chance to rewrite this old fella's story with a happier ending.

With help from the deputy, he soon had the horse settled in the paddock with a pail of water and a flake of hay. Audra and Lindsey pitched in by spreading a bed of fresh shavings beneath the barn roof extension. Spencer placed a call to the vet to schedule the horse's health evaluation and was told he'd be there before day's end. Expressing his satisfaction with the arrangements, Deputy Miller closed the horse trailer and drove away.

Audra had returned to the house, and Lindsey stood with her chin resting on the paddock fence rail. "He looks so sad," she murmured. "Will he make it?"

Spencer came up beside her, close enough to catch the scent of something sweetly floral. He wished he had the right to slip an arm around her waist, or even to take her hand. "Only time will tell. But at least now—thanks to you—he has a fighting chance."

"If you give me some instruction, I'm happy to keep

an eye on him during the day while you're busy working with your dad."

"Mostly he needs good nutrition and a little kindness." A surge of anger squeezed his chest. "The people he was taken from had no clue how to care for a horse. Thought they could stick him in a field and let him fend for himself."

When her hand slid into his, it was all he could do not to tense in surprise. "Ash has you now," she said in a tender tone, "and that's what matters."

Spencer slanted her a crooked smile. "Ash?"

"Yeah. Thinking of how you're saving his life reminded me of a Bible verse my grandma always loved— the one about beauty for ashes. I can't remember how it goes, but it suits him, don't you think?"

"I know the passage you mean. I'll have to read it later." His mouth had gone dry. All he could think about was her nearness and how much he suddenly wanted to kiss her. He tilted his head. "Lindsey…"

She tensed and sidled away. "I'd better get back to the house. I need to follow up with the VA about Uncle Charles's pension benefits, and later I've got to get started trimming hedges and cleaning out flower beds."

"I should get home, too, before my dad has a conniption." Probably too late for that. And way beyond too late for putting a lid on his growing feelings for Lindsey. He cleared his throat. "As soon as I get a break later, I'll come over and start on the barn repairs."

"Great." She was already edging toward the house. "And maybe we could sit down at the computer together with my notes from the attorney and finalize those nonprofit forms."

A gut check made him draw a quick breath. "Yeah,

about that. Are you sure it wouldn't be rushing things? I mean, you're still figuring out whether Audra will even be able to keep the ranch, and if the situation changes—"

"I told you, I fully intend to save the McClement ranch, same as you're determined to save all the horses you can. So no more negative talk. Deal?"

How could he argue in the face of such single-minded optimism? "Yeah, okay. Deal."

"See you later."

The fires of hope kindling within him, he nodded. "See you later."

Chapter Six

With growing confidence about the event venue idea, Lindsey described it to Audra, and her aunt was in complete agreement. Over the next several days, Lindsey could see real progress in her efforts to spruce up the place. The tasks she'd managed so far had been those that didn't require much more investment than muscle and sweat. With help from Audra, she'd trimmed and shaped the shrubbery around the house. They'd raked leaves and added compost to the flower beds. Friends from Audra's church had supplied them with daffodil, crocus and hyacinth bulbs, along with various iris rhizomes. With those in the ground, along with Audra's few perennials that hadn't completely succumbed to neglect, they could look forward to colorful springtime blooms.

Spencer had also come through for them, doing far more than his share of repairs and cleanup around the ranch. Ash was now housed in the barn, and Spencer had moved Cinnamon into the adjacent stall. In addition to caring for his rescues and working for his father, he'd patched the barn roof, replaced the broken stall gate latches, cut down a dead cedar tree, and gotten Lindsey's grandfather's old brush hog working well enough to mow the tangle of overgrowth along the road and driveway.

The house, barn, chapel and other outbuildings desperately needed painting, but purchasing that quantity of paint would be expensive. Lindsey was back to the same crucial point—she needed someone who believed strongly enough in her vision for the ranch that they'd be willing to invest some up-front cash.

In that regard, Spencer's prospects were looking slightly better. He'd officially established his nonprofit organization, with both Lindsey and Audra signing on as New Start Equine Rescue's first two board members. Two days ago, when they'd previewed the website Joella had designed, she'd never seen his smile so wide. The site had gone live yesterday, coinciding with an announcement in the Gabriel Bend *Weekly Tribune*, and moments ago Spencer had texted Lindsey to let her know he'd already received almost one hundred dollars in donations.

She called Joella to share the news. "Spencer said to thank you again for building his website. He couldn't be happier."

"I was glad to create something for a worthy cause." Joella's sigh rasped across the phone connection. "Wish I had the nerve to do what you did and say goodbye to the corporate world."

"It wasn't so much nerve as desperation." Taking a break on the front porch swing, she glimpsed Audra passing the dining room window. "Plus, I had a compelling reason."

"Your aunt. How's it going, by the way?"

"Thanks to the consolidation loan, I've made a good-size dent in her outstanding debts. All except the back taxes, anyway. I sent in a small partial payment, but the county hasn't budged on the tax sale deadline."

"And your plans for an event venue?"

"Slow. Everything takes time and money, and there's still so much work to be done." Lindsey snorted a weak chuckle. "I'm seriously considering forming my own nonprofit so I can solicit donations."

Joella grew silent for a moment. "That's not a half-bad idea, Linds. Not the nonprofit thing, obviously. But how about crowdfunding? There are several websites where you can run a campaign."

"I always thought those things were kind of flaky. I mean, using social media to ask total strangers to fork over money for what may not even be a legitimate cause?"

"Sure, people have been known to scam the system. But if you target individuals and businesses you already have favorable connections with—"

"I don't think so, Jo-Jo. For one thing, Audra would never agree to anything that sounds remotely like charity. She'd insist on paying back every cent."

"How about if you promised to list the donors' names on a plaque?" Joella suggested. "Or maybe thank them with framed photos of your grand opening."

Lindsey still wasn't convinced. "I need to think some more. Christmas is only a week away, and my mom and stepdad are coming in a couple of days." She glimpsed Spencer hoisting himself over the barbed wire at one of the fence posts, and her heart did its usual fluttering every time she saw him. "I'd better go. Let's talk again soon."

After saying goodbye, she tucked her phone into her jeans pocket and started down the porch steps. Spencer caught her eye and waved, but his flat-lipped smile didn't match the excitement she'd expected after his text earlier.

She caught up with him on his way around back. "Great news about the donations."

"Yeah, thanks." He barely slowed his pace.

"Is everything okay?"

"Just a lot going on." His crisp tone suggested there was more to it than that. More flak from his father and grandfather? He headed for the equipment shed. "Can't give you too much time today, but I wanted to finish clearing the trail to the river."

While helping Audra move cattle again a few days ago, Lindsey had come upon the brushy path leading to a bluff overlooking a gently flowing arm of the San Gabriel River. On the far northwest edge of McClement land, it had always been one of the most picturesque spots on the ranch.

She stayed out of the way while Spencer hooked the brush hog to the tractor and made sure everything started. Over the rumble of the tractor motor, she shouted, "I'll ride ahead in the Mule and get the pasture gates for you."

When he lifted a gloved hand in acknowledgment, she climbed into the utility vehicle and pulled in front of the tractor. Parking to the side of the first gate, she hopped out and swung it open. Spencer drove through, then waited while she followed and closed the gate behind them. They repeated the action twice more before entering the stretch of pastureland bordering the river.

While Spencer mowed the trail, Lindsey drove the

Mule ahead, jouncing over the ruts and dodging brambles until she reached the bluff. Even now, amid the fading fall color of oaks and elms dropping the last of their leaves, the beauty took her breath away. Spying her favorite rock for sitting and thinking, she stomped around it a few times to make sure no snakes, spiders or scorpions lay in wait.

A brisk breeze skimmed past her ears as she scooted onto the sun-warmed rock. The scents of river water, oak and cedar were strong here, mixed with the earthy smells Spencer's mowing released. With the roar of the brush hog behind her and the rippling river below, she tipped her face skyward as an unexpected prayer of longing rose within.

God, I need help. Do You have any idea how over-whelmed I feel? What if I fail Audra? What if all I'm doing here is postponing the inevitable?

But no answers came. Was God even listening? Or had He turned his back on her just like her human father had?

The tractor and mower noises grew louder, then abruptly ceased. Lindsey looked over her shoulder to see Spencer ambling her way. He paused, hands on hips, and scanned the view. A murmured "Wow" slipped between his lips. "It's been a while since I was up here."

"Me, too." Lindsey rose and stood beside him. "Am I crazy?" She cast him a questioning frown. "Is this whole event venue idea even going to work?"

Spencer removed his hat and ran his gloved thumb along the brim. "When you first brought it up a couple of weeks ago, I had my doubts. But then you convinced me I could start a nonprofit equine rescue, and now I'm officially in business." He turned to her, his tender gaze irresistible. "I have confidence in you, Lindsey. If this is what you want, don't let anything stop you."

Feelings she'd been fighting since seeing him again the day she'd arrived battled her lungs for breathing space. In a weak attempt to lighten the moment, she asked, "Even your grumpy old grandfather?"

Exhaling sharply, he locked eyes with her. "*Especially* my grumpy old grandfather."

Her thoughts returned to his evasiveness earlier. "Is he still giving you a hard time about hanging out with a McClement?"

"That's only part of it." Spencer angled away, his mouth tight. "My mom was looking at the website with me this morning. She asked how things were going with you and Audra, and we got to talking about your plans. Tito heard the words *event venue* and about blew a gasket."

"Seriously? What business is it of his?"

"He says the extra traffic and commotion will be bad for our horses."

Lindsey scoffed. "That's hogwash."

"I agree. But…" Jaw working, Spencer stared out across the river.

"Why do I get the feeling there's more you aren't telling me?"

"It's nothing you should have to worry about. Just… keep doing what you're doing." He jammed his hat back on his head. "I need to get back. Stay if you want to. I can get the gates."

She started to say it was fine, that she'd be right behind him, but he'd made it pretty clear he didn't want company. Besides, whatever was eating at him most likely had something to do with the feud, and she was beyond frustrated with the whole thing.

Spencer didn't like secrets. He especially didn't like keeping from Lindsey his grandfather's obsession with gaining possession of the McClement land.

Back home after mowing the trail and checking on Cinnamon and Ash, he'd started down the hall toward the bathroom to wash up for lunch when Tito stopped him.

"I need you to drive me into town this afternoon," his grandfather stated. He thrust a crumpled slip of paper at Spencer. "You can pick up these supplies while I attend to my business."

He examined the list, noting several items he'd already stocked up on last week. Rather than start an argument, he said, "I'm happy to take you to town, Tito. But first I should make sure Dad doesn't need me for something."

"My business is more important. Whatever jobs he has for you can wait." His grandfather brushed past him into the small room he used for his private office and slammed the door.

Weird. But then, Tito was known for barking orders without giving reasons.

After washing his hands and changing into a clean shirt, he ambled to the kitchen, where his mother had sandwich fixings on the table. He gave her a quick hug. "Any idea what's going on with Tito? He just ordered me to take him to town."

"Who knows? He's been in his office most of the morning, and the couple of times he did show his face, he was crankier than a cornered coyote."

A few minutes later, his dad came in for lunch, but

...oin them. If Dad knew what Tito was up to,
...o himself. After they finished eating, Spencer
...s mother put things away, then steeled himself
to ...ck on the office door. "Whenever you're ready
to go to town…"

The door swung open. "I'm ready now."

"Sure you don't want some lunch first?"

His grandfather harrumphed. Hat and jacket in hand,
he strode through the kitchen. Spencer hurried to grab
his down vest, hat and keys as he raced to catch up.

Moments later, he steered the truck down the lane.
"Where are we headed?"

His grandfather shot him an annoyed glare. "I told
you. Town."

"I got that much. Farm and ranch supply? Barbershop? Bonnie's Bistro?" Those were Tito's usual hang-
outs where he met up with his ranching pals.

Tito's chin shifted sideways as he stared through the
windshield. "The barbershop will do."

He didn't say another word for the rest of the ride.

Arriving on Central Avenue, Spencer pulled into an
empty space in front of Carl's Clips for Men. "When
should I pick you up?"

"I'll call you when I'm ready." Tito clambered out the
passenger door. Standing on the sidewalk, he watched
as Spencer backed into the street.

Perfect. *When I'm ready* could mean twenty minutes, an hour, three hours—no way of knowing. So
much for the odd jobs and training rides Spencer had
planned for the afternoon. Continuing down Central,
he glanced in the rearview mirror to see his grandfather
striding in the opposite direction from the barbershop.
Yep, the old guy was definitely up to something. Spen-

cer only hoped this didn't have anything to do with fi-
nagling a way to buy the McClement ranch.

At the farm and ranch supply, he edited Tito's list
to only what was needed. That left two replacement
horse blankets, four sets of leg wraps and a bucket of
hoof pellets. He also threw in vitamin supplements and
specialty feed for Cinnamon and Ash. With no call yet
from his grandfather, he headed back downtown for pie
and coffee at Bonnie's Bistro. Almost directly across
the street from the barbershop, Bonnie's would let him
keep an eye out for Tito and possibly catch a glimpse of
which establishment the old man had actually visited.

Pulling into the narrow lot alongside the café, Spencer found a parking space among a dozen or so other
trucks and SUVs. As he rounded the building toward
the entrance, he saw Lindsey leaving the electric co-op
office a few doors down. She turned in his direction
and smiled as their eyes met.

"Hi," she said as he neared. She looked drop-dead
gorgeous in skinny jeans, a teal tunic-length sweater,
and a multicolored scarf tied in a fancy knot. "Thought
you'd be busy with horses this afternoon."

"Should have been, but my grandfather wanted a ride
to town for…something." He peered across the street.
No sign of Tito yet.

Lindsey must have caught his look. Smirking, she
shot one brow skyward. "Afraid he'll catch you fraternizing with a McClement in public?"

Heat flared in Spencer's chest. "He can think whatever he wants."

"I'm teasing you, Spencer." She rolled her eyes, then
muttered, "I think so, anyway. As fast as you took off

this morning, maybe you were worried your gra█ ther had spies in the woods."

"Yeah, that was rude of me. I've…had a lot on ▒ mind."

Her sad-eyed smile said she understood. "Well, as of five minutes ago, I have one less thing on *my* mind." She nodded toward the building behind her. "I just paid Audra's overdue electric bill. We can keep the lights on for one more month."

"That's good news worth celebrating." Spencer fingered a ball of lint in his vest pocket. "I was about to have a slice of Bonnie's award-winning pecan pie while I wait for Tito. Join me? My treat, of course."

Pulling her lower lip between her teeth, she looked as if she was about to say no. Then a tentative grin began to spread. "Your treat, huh? Thanks. I haven't had pie at Bonnie's Bistro in forever."

Pulse quickening as he held the café door for Lindsey, Spencer hoped Tito wouldn't finish his business in town too quickly.

The bistro had open seating for the afternoon, so Spencer looked for an empty table near the front window. He pulled out a chair for Lindsey at a small table for two, then took the seat across from her. A waitress came right over with glasses of water and menus.

"I think we both want pie and coffee." Spencer looked to Lindsey for confirmation.

She nodded. "Pecan pie and decaf for me. And no topping on the pie, please. I like mine plain so I can savor every yummy bite."

"Same for me," Spencer said. He usually liked a scoop of vanilla ice cream with his pie, but Lindsey had a point. Why mess with perfection? Besides, with her

, across from him, life seemed—for this moment,
vay—about as close to perfection as it could be.

The waitress returned shortly with their orders. After
sip of decaf, Lindsey asked, "Noticed any more website traffic?"

"A couple more donations came in today. And thanks
to Audra's enthusiasm in her first blog post, a local
teenager's interested in volunteering on Saturday mornings." Smiling to himself, Spencer forked off a gooey
bite of pie. "I think he may need some community service hours."

"Would that be a bad thing? I mean, can you think of
a better way to heal a troubled teen's heart than spending time with horses?"

The faraway look in her eyes suggested her thoughts
had drifted to the difficult years after her father left.
Spencer's family might have their issues, but he'd always be thankful he'd grown up with two loving parents
committed to working through whatever differences
arose. If only he could hope for a marriage like theirs
someday. If only it could be with Lindsey…

Had he missed the opportunity to be more than a
friend to her? More than the computer-illiterate horse
lover whose grandfather couldn't leave old grudges in
the past?

Shoving such notions aside, he focused on the sugary
bite of pie filling dissolving on his tongue. To think, all
this time he could have been enjoying Bonnie's pecan
pie for the deliciousness it was.

Lindsey tapped his knuckle with the side of her fork.
"Usually when you invite someone for pie and coffee,
it's polite to make conversation."

He released a self-conscious laugh. "Thought you

figured it out ages ago—conversation was ne
strong suit."

"Oh, I remember." Lips in a pinch, she gave her h
a quick shake. "There were plenty of times I wante
to tape Samuel's mouth shut so he'd let you get a word
in edgewise."

He stared at her in surprise.

"Don't look at me like I'm nuts. I've always sensed
there's plenty going on inside your head. Good stuff
worth sharing, if only you'd open up more." She glanced
down abruptly and scooped another forkful of dessert.
"Anyway, I'll shut up now."

"Don't."

"Don't…what?"

"Stop talking. I mean, *don't* stop talking." Mouth
suddenly parched, he gulped his coffee.

A funny smile skewed her lips. "Not sure who's more
nervous and confused here—you or me."

"I win the nervous award hands down."

"So that leaves me taking the prize for confused. Are
we—that is, is there something—" A swallow tracked
up and down her throat. "Because I used to hope—"

Before she could complete the thought, her cell phone
sounded from inside her purse. She squeezed her eyes
shut briefly before taking out the phone. Reading the
display, she grimaced.

"Problem?" Spencer asked, really wishing she hadn't
been interrupted.

The phone kept ringing, an annoying ascending tone
that sounded like a robotic marimba. "It's my dad."

Chapter Seven

Frozen with indecision, Lindsey stared at the phone ringing in her hand. Why else could her father be calling except to pile on more pressure about selling?

"You don't have to talk to him," Spencer said softly.

"I kind of do, since legally, he's half owner of the ranch." Shoulders drooping, Lindsey slid back her chair. "This is bound to turn ugly. I'll take it outside."

She answered the call on her way out of the café. "This isn't the best time, Dad. What do you want?"

"A little politeness wouldn't hurt."

"We're way beyond politeness between us. Have been ever since you turned your back on Mom and me."

Her father huffed. "You're not being fair, Lindsey. There are things…things you don't know."

"Feel free to enlighten me." Spotting a wrought iron bench between the café and the electric co-op, she walked over and plopped down. "Seriously, go ahead. I can't wait to hear what kind of fairy-tale explanations you've dreamed up. And don't you dare try to blame Mom for *your* mistakes."

The static-filled silence made her wonder if they'd

been disconnected. "I'm not getting into this v
right now," her father stated, ice in his tone. "
you're all about getting to the point, I'll make this b
I just got off the phone with Audra's attorney. He sa
the corporation interested in buying the ranch uppec
their offer today. I want you to help me convince Audra
to accept."

Lindsey's mouth fell open. Boiling outrage propelled
her to her feet. "You have some nerve—" At the stares
from passersby, she turned away and lowered her voice.
"Why should you have any say in what we do with the
ranch when you've expressed absolutely *zero* interest
in it until now?"

"Let me make something clear, Linds. *You* are the
one who ultimately has no say in this. The ranch be-
longs equally to Audra and me."

"Equally—right. Which means you both have to
agree. And since I'm here and you're not, I wonder
who's going to have the most influence on your sister."

"I have alternatives." Her father's voice took on a
disquieting edge. "I don't think either you or Audra
want me using them."

"Is that a threat? Because it's not working, and I
don't believe you, anyway." From the corner of her eye,
Lindsey glimpsed Spencer coming her way. A worried
look creased his brow.

"Don't try me, Lindsey," her father said. "Please…"
Tiredness crept in, replacing the chill in his tone. "Try
to be reasonable about this. If you'll put sentimentality
aside and look at it rationally, you'll see that selling is
the only thing that makes sense."

The line went dead.

Spencer moved closer. "You okay?"

m not." Lindsey held the phone away from her
s if it were dripping with poison. "He said I'm
sentimental and irrational. He says he has *alterna-*
es. Which I'm sure means some kind of legal fight."

"I'm sorry, Linds." Gently taking her elbow, Spencer nudged her back to the bench and sat down beside her. "Is there any chance he can change Audra's mind about selling?"

"Most days I'd say no. But if he catches her in a weak moment when she's been dwelling on how bleak things look…" Unshed tears swelled Lindsey's throat. Leaning forward, she shoved stiff fingers through the curls at her temple. "I can't lose our family's ranch. I just can't."

"It'll be okay." His tone firm with conviction, Spencer drew a sheltering arm around her. "Somehow, it'll be okay."

Warmed by his tender protectiveness, she lifted her head to offer a weak smile. "How can you be so sure?"

"Because I know you. And because…" His voice trailed off as his gaze drifted toward the other side of the street.

Straightening, Lindsey glimpsed Arturo Navarro ambling down the sidewalk opposite them. He paused in front of the barbershop, and when he looked their way, a scowl darkened his expression.

Lindsey cast Spencer a mocking frown. "Busted."

When he squared his shoulders and purposefully locked his fingers with hers, she could have keeled over from shock. He shifted slightly to face her. "I need to go. But first, I want you to promise me you won't give up." His grip on her hand tightened. "No matter what."

Before she could find her voice to ask why he cared

so much about saving the ranch of his gra⸱
worst enemy, he was halfway across the street.

At home later—Lindsey wasn't sure when sⱼ
started thinking of the ranch as *home*, but there
was—she couldn't bring herself to mention her father's
phone call. Audra had probably gotten the same update
from the attorney, and when she didn't seem inclined
to broach the subject, Lindsey chose to see it as a positive sign that her aunt hadn't given up yet either.

Besides, they had plenty to do that weekend with
housecleaning and getting another guest room ready
for Lindsey's mom and stepdad, who were expected
Sunday afternoon.

On Saturday morning, Audra stifled a sneeze as she
shook out the heirloom Celtic cross quilt covering the
guest bed. "Your great-grandmother made this with
scraps of fabric she brought from Ireland. It's one of
my favorites."

"It's beautiful." Laying a set of sheets on the mattress,
Lindsey admired the quilt's blue-and-aqua design. "I'd
never have the patience to create something so intricate."

"Maybe not, but you've got all the patience in the
world when it comes to sorting out my financial mess.
And for that," Audra said with a warm smile, "I am
eternally grateful."

With the bed made, Audra went downstairs to start
another load of laundry and work on the grocery list.
Lindsey finished dusting and vacuuming the room, then
made sure there was drawer and closet space for her
mother's and stepdad's things. Next, she tackled the upstairs bathroom. Seemed like she'd done more physical
labor during these three weeks at the ranch than in the

year. Which wasn't a bad thing, but the effort certainly awakened some long-dormant muscles.

The rumble of a vehicle outside the bathroom window drew her attention. Peering through the curtain, Lindsey didn't recognize the blue pickup. Then she saw Spencer leading Cinnamon from her pasture beyond the barn toward a young couple with a boy who looked to be around ten. Deputy Miller pulled in behind the pickup.

A strange mixture of elation and sorrow squeezed Lindsey's heart. Visiting with the sweet little horse every day, she'd grown attached to her. But now, with Cinnamon healed from her injuries and looking so much healthier, she'd soon be ready for adoption. Dropping the sponge and bathroom cleaner on the floor, Lindsey rushed downstairs hoping this wouldn't be her only chance to say goodbye.

At the foot of the back porch steps, she hesitated. Spencer's parting words yesterday in town had sounded almost prophetic, as if he knew something she didn't, and she'd been puzzling over them ever since. But this wasn't the time to ask, so she strove for a cheery smile as she joined the group.

"Is this Cinnamon's new family?" She stroked the horse's sleek neck.

Spencer held the lead rope. "Lindsey, meet the Foxes. They're hoping to adopt Cinnamon for their son, Timothy."

"How exciting!" Lindsey locked eyes with the fair-haired boy, her expression turning serious. "That's a big responsibility. You'll take good care of her, won't you?"

The boy answered with a mile-wide grin. "The best. I've read every single horse book in the library."

"And that's no exaggeration," his father chimed in. Deputy Miller came forward to hand Mr. Fox a clip-

board and pen. "I need you to fill out a little ⸢
and we'll set the wheels in motion."

So Cinnamon wouldn't be leaving today a⸢
a huge relief. Lindsey turned to Spencer. "What ⸢
pens next?"

"The Foxes' barn and pasture setup has to be in
spected and approved. In the meantime, I'll continue
working with Cinnamon to make sure she's a good
match for Timothy's riding skills. If all goes well, they
can take her home in early January, and I'll do a few
follow-up visits to make sure everything's going okay."

"Can I visit her sometimes until then?" Timothy asked.

"Sure," Spencer replied. "Have your parents give
me a call anytime." Tipping back his hat, he lowered
himself to eye level with the boy. "Bring your riding
helmet and I might even let you help me with Cinnamon's training."

"Wow, really? Awesome!"

Lindsey moved aside while the Foxes completed their
arrangements with Spencer and Deputy Miller. When
everyone else had left, Lindsey waited as Spencer returned Cinnamon to the pasture, then followed him over
to Ash's paddock. Watching him run his hands along
the horse's sides, she said, "He looks better every day."

"He's coming along." Spencer moved around the
horse, carefully examining each hoof. "With the changes
to his diet, though, I need to make sure he doesn't de
velop laminitis."

"You amaze me, you know."

Straightening, Spencer cast her a self-conscious
smile. "It's what I do. Nothing amazing about it."

With a deny-it-all-you-want shrug, Lindsey opened
the gate for Spencer to exit the paddock, then latched

m. "Guess you'll be pretty busy with work
y through the holidays."

too busy to pitch in over here. Any thoughts
what you want to tackle next?"

When my mom and stepdad get here, I'm hoping
ney'll help me haul stuff out of the chapel and decide
what's worth keeping—if there's anything after rats and
insects have been in there for who knows how long."

"Always happy to help with the heavy lifting." Spencer gave a quick nod as he turned in the direction of
the Navarro ranch.

"Before you go…" Lindsey moved in front of him.
"Maybe I don't really want to know the answer, but
something you said right before you left yesterday has
been bugging me."

Spencer massaged the palm of his right hand, the
same one he'd been holding hers with yesterday. Her
fingers tingled at the memory. "Oh, yeah? What'd I
say?"

"You told me not to give up. *No matter what.* Like
you knew there could be a reason I'd consider giving
up."

He looked away, lips downturned in a thoughtful
frown. "I'm coming to believe my grandfather would
do almost anything to get his hands on this place. But if
you're able to pay off the back taxes and avoid the foreclosure sale, that will never happen." His gaze locked
with hers. "You have to believe I'm on your side in this,
Linds. I'll do everything I can to help you keep this
ranch in the McClement family."

She studied him. "Why, Spencer? Why *wouldn't* you
want this land for the Navarros?"

Removing his hat, he sidled a few steps away.

"Maybe I'm not being the loyal son and ⸻
should be, but…it seems wrong. The greed. ⸻
ness. I don't think even gaining possession of t⸻
would be enough to erase my grandfather's discon⸻

Spencer hoped his suspicions were unfounded ar⸻
that Tito's business in town yesterday had nothing to do
with making a bid for the McClement ranch. He meant
what he'd said to Lindsey. His grandfather didn't need
more land. He needed a change of heart.

At church the next morning, Spencer prayed for exactly that. With Christmas only days away, how could
Tito not grasp how his spiteful grudge against the McClements was hardening his heart toward the Prince
of Peace?

Afterward, as they filed out of the sanctuary, Spencer's mother wrapped her arm around his waist. "You
looked so serious all through worship. What's on your
mind, son?"

He slowed, allowing his father and grandfather to
move farther ahead. "I hope I'm wrong, but… I'm worried Tito's planning to make trouble for Lindsey."

"This isn't only friendly concern, is it?" She cast
him a smile fraught with meaning. "Your dad and I
have noticed how much time you've been spending next
door—and not just to take care of your rescue horses."

His stomach tensed. "I'm doing my best to stay on
top of my work with the quarter horses."

"And your dad knows that. He may not be so good
at showing it, but he's proud of what you're doing with
the rescues—more than you know. But he walks a fine
line between honoring your grandfather's legacy and

...the day when Navarro Quarter Horses will ...you."

...paused in the narthex, and Spencer glanced ...ere Dad and Tito stood chatting with a couple ...her ranchers. Guess he'd been so focused on get- ...g the job done each day that he hadn't given much ...hought to the future. Not smart, considering Tito was nearing ninety and wouldn't be around too many more years. And Dad, at sixty, might already be thinking to- ward retirement. When the time came, did Spencer even want to take over the family's quarter horse operation?

Not unless the Navarro-McClement feud had been settled once and for all. And definitely not if gaining his inheritance meant Lindsey had to lose hers.

Mom patted his arm. "Didn't mean to get you fret- ting over all that right now. It's almost Christmas." Her eyes sparkled with anticipation. "Oh, honey, with Sam- uel here for a few days, it'll be like old times having you two boys and Lindsey together again."

"Yeah, should be fun." More like a mixed blessing. Spencer looked forward to having his brother home for Christmas. But the idea of competing with his silver- tongued twin for Lindsey's attention? *Not* so fun. Besides, he was already dreading the arguments sure to arise when Tito and Dad started in on Samuel again for choosing a real estate career instead of the family business. Spen- cer respected his brother for following his own path, but did Samuel have any idea how his leaving had doubled the pressure on Spencer to live up to their father's and grandfather's expectations?

With an impatient scowl, Tito waved at them. "Let's go home. I'm hungry."

Spencer and his mother hurried over, and Dad hus-

tled them out the door. "He's in a mood toda[...]
mured. "Let's not make it worse."

"What's going on with Tito, anyway?" Spence[...]

His father answered with a grim shake of his [...]
"Guess we'll all know soon enough."

Passing the McClement ranch as they arrived hom[...]
Spencer noticed an unfamiliar gold sedan parked in
front of the house. A thin, gray-haired man leaned into
the trunk and hauled out two suitcases. Lindsey, her
mother and Audra were heading up the porch steps,
each of them laden with gifts wrapped in shiny Christmas paper. Even from this distance, Spencer could see
the joy in their faces. His hand clenched in a pang of
envy, because no matter what ultimately happened with
the McClement ranch, Lindsey's family would stick
together, loving and supporting one another through
good times and bad.

As for his own family? Loyalty was one thing. Clinging to the past, something else entirely. If the tables
were turned and the McClements were trying to take
back Navarro land, Spencer hated to think what his
grandfather might do in retaliation. He'd likely destroy
the last remnants of respect any of his children and
grandchildren had for him.

Such disconcerting thoughts reminded Spencer that
he'd been out of touch with his twin for too long. After
helping with kitchen cleanup following Sunday lunch,
he carried his phone out to the front porch and called
Samuel. Might be wise to give his brother a heads-up
about the current situation before he got to town.

"Hey, Spence!" Samuel's typical high-energy greeting sounded slightly forced today. "How's it going, bro?"

"Pretty good. You?"

idn't reply right away. "Okay, I guess."

idn't sound convincing."

it. About as convincing as your 'pretty good.'"

el gave a humorless laugh. "We may not see each

er much anymore, but our twin connection's still

etty strong. So spill."

Spencer wouldn't be cornered so easily. Besides, his brother's mood shift had him concerned. Samuel had gone through a rough patch a year or two ago, and Spencer hoped he hadn't fallen back in with the toxic singles crowd he'd been hanging with. "Uh-uh. You first."

Another pause. "Got time to meet me for coffee later at the Cadwallader Inn?"

"You're in Gabriel Bend?" Stunned, Spencer pushed up from the porch step and took several strides across the lawn. "Since when?"

"Got in last night," Samuel replied sheepishly. "Took the whole week off for Christmas but couldn't make myself go straight to the ranch. Don't tell anyone, though. Promise?"

"You know Mom's gonna kill you when she finds out."

"Won't be the first time. So, can you come to town or not?"

"Be there in half an hour."

Telling his mother only that he'd forgotten something he needed in town, Spencer headed to the Cadwallader. In a quiet corner of the inn's upscale restaurant, he found his brother sipping decaf from a fancy china cup. Now that Samuel had started growing a beard, seeing him was almost like looking in a mirror.

Samuel rose to greet him with a manly hug and a

couple of rough slaps on the back. "Good Spiny."

"You, too, Slam." It had been a long time since used their childhood nicknames, bestowed when were too young to correctly pronounce each othe given names.

As they took chairs opposite each other, Samuel signaled a server. Amused by the young man's double take upon seeing his customer's identical twin, Spencer ordered decaf for himself, then let Samuel run with the small talk until the server returned with another cup and saucer along with a thermal carafe for the table.

Grinning, Samuel topped off his coffee. "I can always tell when you're done with the chitchat. Ready to tell me what's really going on with you?"

"Wait, *you* were supposed to go first with the true confessions."

"Never agreed to that. Anyway, since Mom already sort of filled me in, you might as well fess up."

Spencer nearly choked on a swallow of decaf. "What exactly did Mom tell you?"

"That you've been spending a lot of time with a certain attractive McClement."

Fighting for composure, Spencer mopped his lips with a napkin. "Lindsey and I are working together on a couple of projects, that's all."

"I've seen your horse rescue website. Mom sent me the link. Nice going, by the way. But stabling your horses at the McClement ranch? How's that going over with Tito?"

Not a subject Spencer wanted to get into. "I'm sure you can guess."

"Right. So tell me more about Lindsey."

...d familiar prickles crawled up Spencer's
...nce you're so interested, why don't you go
...e and see her?"

...aning away, Samuel raised both hands. "Easy, bro.
.. trying to move in on your girl."

"She's not my—"

"It's okay, Spiny." Samuel shifted forward, forearms
resting on the table. His expression softened into a sympathetic smile. "I've known you were sweet on Lindsey
since junior high."

"But I always thought you—I mean, the way you
were always flirting with her—"

Samuel scoffed. "Because you weren't. And it wasn't
really flirting. Not seriously, anyway. Lindsey was just
fun to be with."

"Still is," Spencer murmured, gazing toward the window but seeing only a pair of shimmering brown eyes.

"Yep, my brother is smitten." Samuel sat back with
a satisfied smirk. "And it's about time you finally admitted it."

Chapter Eight

Lindsey had helped Audra set out a few Christmas decorations over the past week, but with ranch business taking precedence, they hadn't gotten around to putting up a tree. After carrying in all the gifts her mother and stepdad had brought, Lindsey suggested they go into town that afternoon and pick one out.

"The best tree lot's next to Jim's Food Mart," Audra said. "Y'all go find us a nice one, and I'll have the lights and ornaments ready when you get back."

Driving Audra's ancient blue ranch truck, Lindsey headed into Gabriel Bend with her mother and Stan. This close to Christmas, many of the best trees had already been claimed, but they found a nicely shaped six-foot Douglas fir perfect for a corner in Audra's living room. Stan insisted on paying for it, and while he and the lot attendant secured it in the truck bed, Lindsey jogged to the food mart to pick up a few things Audra needed for supper.

As she approached the self-checkout with her basket of cherry tomatoes, salad greens and dinner rolls, the person ahead of her had just finished bagging his

s. When he turned slightly, she saw it was ...—and wearing a long-sleeved polo and khakis ... nicer than his usual attire. "Hey, stranger," she ... with a laugh. "Almost didn't recognize you with- ...t your jeans and Stetson."

He pivoted to face her, his mouth spreading into a grin. "Hi, Lindsey. Don't tell me you still can't tell my brother and me apart."

Her jaw dropped. "Samuel?"

Grocery bag looped over one arm, he gave her a quick hug with the other. "Been forever, huh? How are you?"

"I—I'm good. You're home for Christmas?"

He squeezed one eye shut in an embarrassed grimace. "The fam's not expecting me till Christmas Eve. I needed a couple days to myself, so I'm staying at the Cadwallader."

"They don't know you're in town?"

"Only Spencer. And I'd like to keep it that way... for now."

"No worries." Her smile stiffened. "I'm not exactly on speaking terms with your dad and grandfather."

Samuel gave his head a disgusted shake. "This whole Navarro-McClement thing stinks. What it's done to my family is a big reason I left home in the first place—and why it's so hard to come back even for a short visit."

His admission made her sad for him and even angrier about the feud. "Well, I know Spencer will be glad to see you."

"He met me for coffee at the inn earlier. We had a good talk." Samuel winked. "Actually, we mostly talked about you."

Heat rose in Lindsey's cheeks. At someone's em-

phatic throat-clearing behind her, she apologi[...]
hurried to scan her groceries. Samuel bagged the[...]
her and waited while she ran her debit card, then wa[...]
her out. By then, her stepdad had moved the truck to[...]
parking space near the exit doors.

"Well, I should go," she said, still feeling the warmth
of her blush. "We're decorating our tree this afternoon."

"It's good to see you again, Lindsey. For my brother's
sake, I hope you stick around Gabriel Bend for a long,
long time."

His statement awakened a swarm of butterflies in
her stomach. What exactly had Spencer told him? With
an uncertain smile, she said goodbye and strode over
to the truck.

When she climbed in on the passenger side, her
mother asked, "Was that Spencer?"

"No, it was Samuel." Lindsey explained his request
not to mention his arrival in town. Not that Mom and
Stan were any more likely to speak with Arturo or Hank
Navarro than she was. But when Mrs. Navarro learned
Lindsey's mother was visiting, she'd probably pop over
to say hello in spite of her crusty old father-in-law.

At the ranch, Lindsey helped Stan carry the Christmas tree inside. Audra had the stand ready, and soon
they were stringing lights and hanging ornaments. Discovering they needed an extension cord, Audra sent
Lindsey to the storage closet to find one. On her way
back to the living room, she drew up short at the sight
of her mother and stepdad stealing a kiss. The tender
gaze they shared brought a lump to Lindsey's throat.
She couldn't be happier that Mom had found true love
again, and with such a kind and gentle man.

Just as quickly, those tender feelings evaporated as

...ghts jumped to her father. He didn't deserve
...ness, much less the forgiveness Mom had long
...chosen to give. Lindsey couldn't forgive him and
...ver would.

"There you are, honey." Mom's cheeks glowed as
she eased out of Stan's embrace. "Let's get these lights
plugged in, shall we?"

For the remainder of the day, Lindsey put her nega-
tivity aside and let herself enjoy this time with her family. Mom and Stan were enthusiastic about Lindsey's
ideas to generate other sources of income for the ranch
and promised to pitch in with some of the cleanup and
fixing up during their stay.

The next morning, after helping Audra with the barn
and livestock chores, Lindsey decided the mild, sunny
weather was perfect for starting to clear out the chapel.
"Who knows? There might actually be something worth
salvaging in there."

Mom peered through the open door. "It'll be like a
treasure hunt. And you know how I love antiquing."

"Watch for snakes and spiders," Audra cautioned as
she donned a pair of leather work gloves. "You're right,
though. Several years ago I helped my parents move
some ancient boxes and furniture down from the attic
that the original owners had left behind."

By noon, the area outside the chapel was strewn
with rotting cardboard crates, an antique trunk with
rusty hinges and an assortment of mismatched furniture, some of which showed signs of rodent damage.

Lindsey groaned as she surveyed the piles. "So much
for finding anything of value."

"Don't give up so quickly," Mom said, already rif-
fling through the trunk. She lifted out an old book, then

sat back on her heels and gingerly turned to the flyleaf. "This looks like a first-edition Mark Twain novel, and it's still in pretty good shape."

Stan stooped to examine the page. "If you're right, it could be worth several hundred dollars. Maybe thousands."

"Are you serious?" Heart pounding, Lindsey hurried over to peer inside the trunk. "Are there more?"

"A few, but they don't look as well preserved as this one." Mom handed the book to Stan, then lifted out another volume. "We need to get these appraised."

Audra joined them, her eyes wide with interest. "I know an antiques dealer in town."

Ready to burst with excitement, Lindsey drew her aunt into a hug. "I have a good feeling about this. Can we call him right now?"

"I'll go find his number." Audra started toward the house.

"Bring some tissue paper back with you," Mom called. "We should carefully wrap each book until a professional can tell us for sure what we've got."

As Lindsey knelt to see what else the trunk held, she glimpsed Spencer ambling toward the barn. Seeing them, he changed direction and headed over. "You've been busy."

"Seemed like a good day to get started on the chapel." Lindsey stood and brushed debris from her knees. "You remember my mom."

"Sure. Hi, Mrs..."

"Aaronson," Lindsey's mother supplied. "And this is Stan, my husband." She laughed lightly. "We thought for a second we'd seen you at the grocery store yesterday, but it turned out to be your brother."

Spencer cast Lindsey a nervous glance. "You saw Samuel?"

"Don't worry. He told us not to say anything."

"Uh…good. Thanks." His distracted reply made Lindsey wonder if he had other reasons to be concerned they'd run into his twin. "Just came over to check on my rescues. If you need help hauling this stuff off later, let me know."

Lindsey debated whether she should mention their find and risk the possibility of word getting back to his grandfather. If Arturo thought they had any chance of paying off the ranch debts, no telling what shenanigans he might try.

Audra scurried toward them, a package of tissue paper in one hand and a cordless phone in the other. "I have Alan Picton on the phone. He'd love to take a look— Oh, hi, Spencer. Did Lindsey tell you what we found?"

"Haven't had a chance yet." Avoiding Spencer's questioning stare, Lindsey grabbed the tissue paper. "Maybe we should, um…" She hoped her aunt would catch the meaning behind her pointed glance.

Audra nodded and lifted the phone to her ear. "Hi, Alan. I'm going to let you talk to my sister-in-law. She knows more about these things than I do."

Lindsey's mother took the phone and moved several feet away. Lindsey handed the tissue paper to her stepdad, then motioned Spencer to walk with her toward the barn. "Please promise you'll keep this to yourself."

Spencer snorted. "Seems like I'm doing a lot of that lately. What exactly is going on?"

She told him about the books and the hope they could be valuable. "Even a few hundred dollars could be our seed money to get the event venue up and running. Or if

Complete the survey below and return it today to receive up to 4 FREE BOOKS and FREE GIFTS guaranteed!

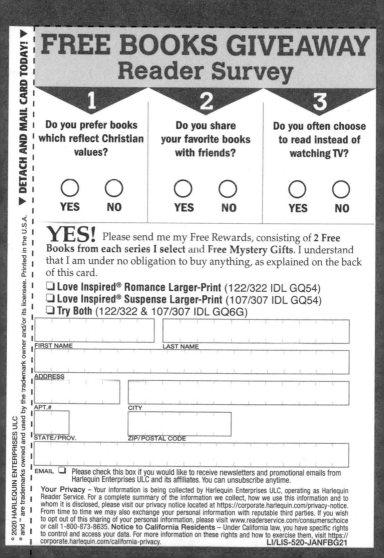

▼ DETACH AND MAIL CARD TODAY! ▼

FREE BOOKS GIVEAWAY
Reader Survey

1

Do you prefer books which reflect Christian values?

○ YES   ○ NO

2

Do you share your favorite books with friends?

○ YES   ○ NO

3

Do you often choose to read instead of watching TV?

○ YES   ○ NO

YES! Please send me my Free Rewards, consisting of **2 Free Books from each series I select** and **Free Mystery Gifts**. I understand that I am under no obligation to buy anything, as explained on the back of this card.

❏ Love Inspired® Romance Larger-Print (122/322 IDL GQ54)
❏ Love Inspired® Suspense Larger-Print (107/307 IDL GQ54)
❏ Try Both (122/322 & 107/307 IDL GQ6G)

| FIRST NAME | LAST NAME |

| ADDRESS |

| APT.# | CITY |

| STATE/PROV. | ZIP/POSTAL CODE |

EMAIL ❏ Please check this box if you would like to receive newsletters and promotional emails from Harlequin Enterprises ULC and its affiliates. You can unsubscribe anytime.

HARLEQUIN READER SERVICE—**Here's how it works:**

▲ If offer card is missing write to: Harlequin Reader Service, P.O. Box 1341, Buffalo, NY 14240-8531 or visit www.ReaderService.com ▲

BUSINESS REPLY MAIL

FIRST-CLASS MAIL   PERMIT NO. 717   BUFFALO, NY

POSTAGE WILL BE PAID BY ADDRESSEE

HARLEQUIN READER SERVICE
READER SERVICE
PO BOX 1341
BUFFALO NY 14240-8571

NO POSTAGE
NECESSARY
IF MAILED
IN THE
UNITED STATES

they're worth a lot more, maybe we could pay off *all* Aunt Audra's debts and she could get back into ranching."

Reaching the paddock, Spencer clucked to Ash to call him over, then grew silent as he stroked the horse's neck. "That'd be great news for all of you," he murmured, a frown belying his words. "I expect you're counting the days till you can get back to your own life."

An automatic *yes* sprang to her lips, but she snapped her mouth shut before it escaped. With every day she spent on the ranch, the idea of leaving Gabriel Bend to return to corporate finance lost more and more of its appeal.

At the twinge in his gut, Spencer could only nod when Lindsey abruptly excused herself to deal with the stuff they'd hauled out of the old chapel. She'd responded to his remark with little more than a shrug, and he ached for something he could say that would keep her in Gabriel Bend, because the longer she stuck around, the harder it would be to see her go.

Best to turn his attention to what he knew best—horses. After giving Ash and Cinnamon each a thorough grooming, he saddled Cinnamon for a short ride. The mare was a quick learner and longed to please. She'd make an excellent first horse for Timothy Fox and might even go home with him sooner than originally planned.

Heading home later, he glanced toward the pasture where Audra's horses grazed. Flash's Navarro brand still intrigued him, as did the fact that his father had quietly made a gift of the horse to Charles Forrester. If only this act of kindness meant the differences between the two families would someday be resolved.

Dad was unmerciful with Spencer that afternoon,

though, handing him a long list of tasks involving the quarter horses. "And make sure Dazzle is ready for Jenny Thomas. She's coming for her tomorrow at ten."

The barrel-racing mare was more than ready. When Jenny arrived the next morning, Spencer had the horse warmed up in the round pen. Jenny had brought her own saddle and tacked Dazzle for a trial run. Crossing the finish line, the girl was grinning like crazy.

"She's the whole package," Jenny said, leaping to the ground. "Speed, agility, willingness. I can't wait to enter her in competition."

"Be sure to let us know how she does." Spencer allowed himself a moment of pride in his training, along with renewed appreciation for the quality bred into the Navarro horses.

As Jenny led Dazzle from the arena, a shiny red Mazda drove up. "Finally. I didn't think my fiancé was going to make it." She waved as a lanky guy in stiff indigo jeans unfolded himself from the car. "Hey, honey, where've you been? You missed my ride."

"Sorry, I got lost finding the place." The man strode over and offered Jenny a quick kiss, then turned to Spencer for a handshake. "Zach Muñoz. So, you're the famed horse trainer I've been hearing about."

"That'd be a stretch." Spencer dipped his chin.

Jenny handed Zach the horse's reins. "Take her for me, hon? I need to grab my checkbook and settle up with Spencer."

In the barn office, Spencer tried not to look too incompetent while bringing up her account on the computer. After locating it, he handed her a slip of paper with the balance due, then waited as she wrote out a check.

Exhaling loudly, she passed the check across the

desk. "With a million and one wedding expenses coming up, I have no business spending money on a horse right now, but I couldn't wait."

An idea niggling, Spencer chewed his lower lip. "When's the big day?"

"We're thinking June, after Zach finishes at UT. But the venues we've checked so far are booked solid through the summer."

"I might know of a place." He hoped he wasn't speaking out of turn. "It's new, but they should be ready in plenty of time for a June wedding."

Jenny's eyes lit up. "Really? Where?"

"Right next door. My friend's getting ready to open an event venue. There's even an old family chapel they're planning on fixing up."

"I'd love to see it. Do you think they'd have time to talk to us today?"

"I'll text my friend and ask."

Seconds later, Lindsey fired back a reply, complete with three thumbs-up emoji and a smiley face. YES!!! Send them right over!!! I'll meet them out front.

Relaying the message, Spencer offered to go along and make the introductions. He helped Jenny get Dazzle into the trailer, then took his usual shortcut across the barbed-wire fence while Jenny and her fiancé drove their vehicles. He reached Lindsey as she made her way down the front steps.

Her bright smile stretched wide. "I can't believe this—a possible client already!"

"Haven't I been telling you to have faith?"

"I know, but...some days definitely make it easier than others."

Jenny pulled up in her SUV, and her fiancé parked

his Mazda behind the horse trailer. Hand in hand, they ambled over. Spencer introduced them to Lindsey.

"We still have a lot of work to do," Lindsey said, leading the way around the side of the house, "but I hope you'll be able to see the potential. So, you're planning a June wedding?"

Watching Lindsey transition into full-on business mode, exuding confidence even when Spencer suspected part of it was pretense, he admired her all the more. After turning Jenny and Zach over to Lindsey, he should have excused himself and headed back to work, but his fascination wouldn't let him. Besides, as a member of the cleanup crew, he had a small stake in this venture, or so he'd like to believe.

At the chapel, now empty of everything that had been stored there, Lindsey described her plans for sprucing it up inside and out. She paused, a fingertip to her chin. "By the way, have you had your engagement photos taken yet?"

"That's next on our to-do list," Jenny said. "I wanted to wait until I brought Dazzle home so she could be in the photos with us."

Lindsey beamed. "I love that idea."

"And if you're looking for the perfect backdrop…" With a meaningful glance at Lindsey, Spencer motioned toward the equipment shed. "If you have time, we could hop in the Mule and Lindsey can show you one of the most picturesque spots on the ranch."

When Jenny and Zach shared let's-do-it nods, Lindsey shot Spencer a vibrant smile of thanks. A few minutes later, the four of them climbed into the four-wheeler. With Lindsey driving and Spencer hopping out to open and shut gates, they were soon at the river overlook.

Stepping to the ground, Jenny sucked in a delighted gasp. "It's gorgeous—exactly the kind of natural setting I'd been picturing." She squeezed Zach's hand. "What do you think, honey?"

"You're right, babe, it's perfect." The spindly groom-to-be turned to Lindsey. "Can we coordinate with our photographer for right after the first of the year?"

"Sure. Just give me a call." Spencer could tell Lindsey was ready to burst, but she disguised it well.

"Got a business card?" Zach asked.

Lindsey grimaced. "Sorry, not yet. Still waiting on the print order."

Spencer felt pretty sure she hadn't even thought of ordering business cards yet, but he was glad to have given her a reason to. For now, she did some fancy thing with her phone that transferred her contact info to Jenny's. On the way back in the Mule, Jenny bubbled over with ideas she and Zach had been discussing for the wedding, and Lindsey promised to make some notes and start a file for them right away.

Once the couple said goodbye and had driven away in their separate vehicles, Lindsey released a long, shaky breath. "I think I'm in shock. Do you think they'll actually commit?"

"Why wouldn't they?" Spencer laughed. Crazy, how badly he wanted to kiss her. "You completely sold them, Linds."

"All thanks to you. I can't wait to tell Audra." Brows shooting skyward in a sudden look of panic, she pressed both hands to her cheeks. "What am I thinking? I can't possibly pull this off without help. And besides—*June*?

What if I land a job somewhere else by then? This was *my* pie-in-the-sky scheme to save the ranch. I can't dump it all on Audra and then leave."

Spencer could have seen this coming a mile away, but at least he hadn't been living in denial the way Lindsey had. Growing serious, he tilted his head. "If moving on was always your plan, how exactly did you see this playing out?"

"I don't know." She sank onto the porch step. "Guess I never let myself think that far ahead."

He stood in front of her, feet planted apart and hands on hips. "Maybe it's time you did."

Spencer was right—Lindsey had focused so closely on the day-to-day details that she hadn't looked too hard into the future. Much as she loved the ranch, staying on permanently had never been her intention. Not to mention that doing so would be totally unrealistic. She was a finance professional, not a rancher. And definitely not an experienced event coordinator.

She looked up at Spencer and sighed. "I need a better plan."

The front door opened, and her mother joined them. "How'd the meeting go?"

"They're interested," Lindsey said, pushing tiredly to her feet. "Now I have to figure out how to coordinate a spectacular June wedding when I have no idea what I'm doing."

"June? That's months away." Mom waved her hand. "You've got this, Linds. Besides, you told me you'd already talked with Holly and Joella about your event venue ideas. They'll give you all the advice you need."

"What I *need* is for them to move to Gabriel Bend

ASAP so I can hire them to take over and run the show." She winced at how whiny she sounded.

Spencer's frown said he'd heard it, too. He shuffled backward. "I should get going. Y'all have a lot to work out." He turned to go, then paused and looked straight into Lindsey's eyes. "Whatever happens, whatever you need, I'll be here."

His reassurance pierced her heart. Before she could find the words to thank him, he was halfway across the field.

"I've always liked him," Mom said, then added under her breath, "despite his grandfather." Brightening, she reached for Lindsey's hand. "Come on inside, honey. Audra's antiques expert called back a few minutes ago."

All other thoughts vanishing, Lindsey followed her mother to the kitchen, where Audra stirred a pot of soup on the stove. "What did he say?" Lindsey blurted. "Is it good news?"

"Let's put it this way." Audra cast an enigmatic smile over her shoulder. "It's not exactly disappointing." She stated the figure she'd been quoted.

Lindsey staggered to the nearest chair. "That—that's nearly half of your back taxes."

"And he's only talking about the book that's in the best condition. The others have value, too, although not nearly as much." Taking a stack of soup bowls from the cupboard, Audra went on, "Alan knows someone who may be interested in buying the books, but he won't be able to reach him until after the holidays."

Mom hugged Lindsey. "See, honey? Have faith. Things are looking up."

Thoughts spinning, Lindsey pulled herself together enough to help get lunch on the table. This close to

Christmas, she wouldn't make much headway with the county tax office. After the first of the year, though—and if Audra's antiques friend came through for them—maybe Lindsey could convince the county to accept a big enough partial payment to forestall the tax sale proceedings and grant them a little more time to pay off the balance.

Time to turn the ranch into a moneymaking event venue. Time to hire the right people to keep it running.

Time to figure out where her life was headed.

Have faith? If only it were as easy as Mom and Audra and Spencer implied. Lindsey was still trying to find her faith, crushed so long ago when her father walked out and turned her young life upside down. Her college decision to major in finance had become her way of making things add up again, figuratively and literally. Numbers didn't lie. One plus one always equaled two.

Church sermons and Sunday school classes had driven home another lesson, this one from the book of Luke, if memory served her correctly. When making plans to build a tower, one should count the cost to ensure there was enough to finish it, or else risk being mocked as a failure. Lindsey understood the spiritual truths implicit in the passage—that following Jesus required full commitment. But practically speaking, it was one more reminder that she needed to determine sooner rather than later what her role would be in the future of the McClement ranch.

Chapter Nine

It wasn't until the Christmas Eve candlelight service that Spencer saw his brother again. He didn't know for sure how Samuel had been occupying himself while staying at the Cadwallader Inn, but the few times they'd spoken by phone that week gave him the impression Samuel was using the holiday downtime to do some hard thinking.

Maybe one of these days his twin would open up about whatever was weighing on him—if only Sam would ever stick around long enough. With busy lives and a big chunk of Texas separating them, staying in touch got harder all the time.

Samuel walked in five minutes after worship began, which spared an immediate confrontation with Dad and Tito. That didn't stop either one of them from shooting him annoyed glares, but with Spencer and his mother as buffers, they made it through the service without an unpleasant scene.

Christmas morning was another story. Mom had just taken her cranberry-walnut scones out of the oven when Tito, speaking in rapid-fire Spanish, lit into Samuel about being a traitor to the family.

"Stop. Right now." Mom leveled her index finger at Tito's nose. "If you can't put away your bitterness even on the day celebrating our Lord's birth—"

"You don't have to defend me, Mom." Samuel pushed away from the breakfast table. "The old man can say whatever he likes about me. I'm leaving."

"Sam, no." Spencer grabbed his brother's arm. "It's Christmas. Come on. Both of you," he added with a pointed stare at his grandfather.

Hand pressed against the center of his chest, Tito inhaled slowly. "All I have ever wanted," he began, his voice oddly quiet, "all I have ever worked for is to secure the Navarro legacy for my heirs." His gaze shifted between Spencer and Samuel. "For *both* my grandsons."

Spencer slanted a brow. His grandfather surely hadn't meant to exclude Aunt Alicia and Uncle David's son? Six years older than Spencer and Samuel, their cousin Mark had grown up in Montana, closer to where Uncle David's family was from. He hadn't spent much time at the ranch, but he was as much an heir as Spencer and Samuel.

Tito must not be thinking clearly, that was all. Dad had expressed concern about the elderly man's health lately. Probably not the best time to bring it up, though. Spencer's immediate priority was keeping his twin from storming out before they could spend what was left of the Christmas holiday together.

"Sit down, Slam, please?" He offered his most persuasive grin. "You know you love Mom's Christmas scones as much as I do."

With a sidelong glance at their grandfather, Samuel relaxed into his chair. "Okay, Spiny, for you and Mom," he muttered. "But one more—"

"There won't be," Mom stated. "Hank, honey, if you'd offer grace…"

Dad's typical short and sweet breakfast blessing seemed even pithier than usual, as if the tension around the table had short-circuited his thankfulness and his Christmas spirit.

Spencer could relate. Something was definitely different about this Christmas. Yes, they'd had more than a few tense holidays over the years, especially when Samuel made one of his intentionally brief visits. But this year, a crackle filled the air, a sense that one ill-timed word or thoughtless act could set off an explosion that would damage the family beyond repair.

Was it all related to what was happening next door? It seemed like Tito's increasing obsession with the Mc-Clement ranch had kicked into overdrive not long after Lindsey showed up. Such thoughts stole any enjoyment from the bite of scone Spencer had just taken, turning it to dry, tasteless crumbs on his tongue. He washed it down with a gulp of coffee, then finished the rest so as not to disappoint his mother.

After breakfast, Mom shepherded them into the living room, where piles of wrapped gifts lay scattered beneath the Christmas tree. With Tito holding silent court from his distressed-leather easy chair and ottoman, Mom directed the gift opening until all that remained was an untidy mound of discarded paper, boxes and bows.

Spencer fingered the crown of the new black felt Stetson he'd admired in Lang's Western Wear & Saddle Shop. "This is perfect, Mom. Thanks."

With a sidelong grin, Samuel plopped his matching

hat on his head. "Can you believe, after all these years, Mom's still trying to dress us alike?"

"Big-city Texas real estate professionals wear Stetsons, too," Mom said with a feigned pout. "Hey, we need pictures." She reached for her phone and ordered the twins to pose together in front of the tree.

After several shots—some serious, most downright silly—Spencer called time-out. "Gotta go check on my rescues. Want to come, Sam?"

"Let's go." His brother was five steps ahead of him on the way to the back door.

Which left Spencer to endure his grandfather's disapproving scowl. Well, Tito could get over himself.

Sliding his arms into his down vest, he caught up with Samuel halfway to the barbed-wire fence. "Couldn't get out of there fast enough, huh?"

"My mask of frivolity was wearing thin. And really?" Samuel thumped the underside of his hat brim. "What are we, ten years old again? Surprised Mom didn't also gift us matching cowboy shirts with red bandannas."

"Ease up, will you? It's just a hat." Hoping to lighten the moment, Spencer blocked his brother and struck a macho stance. "Anyway, you have to admit, we look pretty good in these Stetsons."

"Can't argue that." Samuel segued into the mirror image routine they'd perfected as kids, precisely imitating each other's exaggerated motions and facial expressions.

A minute later, they were laughing and bumping shoulders. "We've still got it," Spencer said. He held up his closed fist toward his brother. "Twin power."

"Twin power." Samuel tapped his knuckles to Spencer's. As they started walking again, a note of melancholy returned to his tone. "Kinda sorry we ever had to grow up."

They reached the fence, and Spencer grabbed a post to lever himself over. Samuel followed, and they continued across the field toward the McClement barn. Spencer would have tried again to get his brother to open up about whatever was eating at him, but he glimpsed Lindsey coming out of the house. She paused, arms folded, and drew a huge gulp of air before brushing something from her cheek.

A tear?

A surge of protectiveness quickened his pace. As he neared, she strode to the small pasture where Ash and Cinnamon grazed. Both horses ambled over to accept her behind-the-ear scratches.

"Merry Christmas, Lindsey," he called, hoping not to startle her.

She turned with a quick smile and an unmistakable sheen in her eyes. "Hi, Spencer. Merry Christmas. Oh, and Samuel, too." The slightest tremor tinged her tone. "Have y'all had a good visit?"

Grinning, Samuel tipped his hat. "It just got a hundred times better."

Spencer tamped down a flare of annoyance. Leave it to his brother to turn on the charm when clearly Lindsey was upset about something. "Didn't mean to intrude. We're here to tend the horses."

"You're no intrusion, Spencer." She sniffed. "I needed a breath of fresh air, that's all."

He ran a thumb down his jaw. "I was thinking about saddling Cinnamon for a little exercise and training. Want to be my designated rider?"

"I'd love it!" A genuine sparkle lit Lindsey's eyes, and Spencer warmed to think he'd put it there.

An instant later, he caught the subtle change in his twin's mood. Lips flattened, Samuel palmed his new felt Stetson and eyed it as if contemplating tossing it in the nearest trash bin. "Looks like y'all have this covered," he said, backing off. "Think I'll say my goodbyes at home and head on back to Houston."

"Sam—" Spencer reached toward his brother.

"I need to get going. I'll give you a call one of these days." Pivoting, Samuel took off across the field.

Lindsey came up beside Spencer. "Did I cause that?"

"No, something else is going on with him that he won't talk about." He shifted, meeting her gaze with a probing stare. "Will you tell me what's going on with you?"

"Oh, just the usual angst over how I'm going to save this ranch. Mom and Stan have helped so much, but they have to leave in a couple of days, and I'm still overwhelmed with everything that needs to be done."

"How many times have I told you? I'll do anything I can to help."

"Even with problems of your own? I can see how worried you are about your brother. When I ran into him in town the other day, he wasn't his usual confident self."

Confidence. Exactly what had been missing in Samuel's attitude. Was he struggling with career setbacks? Girlfriend issues? Or, after all this time, was he second-guessing his decision to walk away from the ranch?

Watching his brother scale the fence, Spencer gave his head a quick shake, then turned abruptly and started for the barn. "Come on, let's get Cinnamon saddled for you."

* * *

Lindsey had often wondered what made Samuel choose a big-city career over his father and grandfather's successful quarter horse business.

Same as she'd wondered again and again how her father could walk away from the McClement ranch and everything Grandpa had worked to build here.

The feud, of course, was the easy explanation. But when family ties weren't enough to keep someone close despite disagreements and difficulties, what was left worth holding on to?

Those thoughts made it even harder to say goodbye to her mother and stepdad when they prepared to leave the following Monday morning. She'd hoped they'd change their minds and stay through New Year's Day, but Stan, a telecommunications consultant, had a work commitment in Florida.

"I'm so proud of you, honey." Standing next to the car, Mom drew Lindsey into a hug. "You're doing a great job."

"Thanks, Mom. I hope it turns out to be enough."

"Hey, you've already got an engagement photo shoot scheduled for after the holidays. Plus any day now Audra should hear from her antiques guy about a buyer for those books."

"Connie," Stan said, giving Lindsey's mother a gentle pat on the shoulder, "we need to hit the road."

"I know, I know." Using the pad of her thumb, Mom flicked away the moisture slipping down Lindsey's cheek, then turned to Audra. "Take care of my sweet girl for me."

"You know I will." Audra gave Lindsey's mother a squeeze, then lowered her voice to a conspiratorial whisper. "But in case you didn't notice, she's the one taking care of me."

Minutes later, Lindsey and Audra stood with their arms around each other as Stan backed the car around and headed toward the road. Once they'd driven out of sight, Lindsey blew out a fluttery sigh. "I miss them already."

"It was a lovely Christmas. I'm so glad they could come." Audra steered Lindsey up the porch steps. "How about another warm slice of my Danish coffee cake to cheer us up?"

"Maybe later. I should get back to work on the business card design so we can get those ordered. And there's a little more sprucing up I'd like to do before Jenny and her fiancé bring their photographer next week." Those and a million other tasks were vying for space in Lindsey's brain. Better to keep busy than dwell on the doubts she couldn't seem to shake.

Because one huge dilemma remained—what would happen to all her effort and planning when the time came to move on?

With her laptop open on Charles's desk, she nudged a stylized oak tree graphic around a business card template. Disappointed with the effect, she deleted the graphic and tried one of a steepled church. That one didn't look right, either.

"Face it, girl," she muttered with a groan. "Graphic design is not your forte."

Time to use her phone-a-friend option. Soon Joella was on the line. "I need help."

Joella burst out laughing. "Merry Christmas and Happy New Year to you, too!"

"Sorry, I've been slightly preoccupied." She brought

her friend up-to-date since their last conversation, then explained about needing a business card. "I think we'll call ourselves River Bend Events and Wedding Chapel."

"I like it. Sure, I'm happy to come up with some ideas for you."

"Thanks, Jo-Jo. I hope I haven't intruded on any holiday plans."

"Not here." A weary sigh whispered through the phone. "Holidays aren't the same since Mom died."

Lindsey's heart clenched. Her friend's mother, a victim of early-onset Alzheimer's, had passed away two years ago. "If this isn't a good time—"

"No, it's fine. In fact, I've needed a change of pace so badly that I turned over all my New Year's Eve parties to my in-house associates."

Hearing notes of discontent in Joella's tone, Lindsey chewed her lip. "How serious are you about getting out of corporate event planning?"

"It's…been on my mind."

"If you really are thinking about making a change, I sure could use your expertise to get our little operation up and running. You could even live right here at the ranch—the house has plenty of extra rooms." She paused. "Of course, I can't offer any guarantees about how soon—or even if—we'll turn a profit."

Joella remained silent so long that Lindsey wondered if the connection had dropped. Then her friend blew out sharply. "Oh, Linds, you have no idea how tempting that sounds. And it isn't that I'm worried the venue won't be a success. I'm more concerned you'll be moving on eventually to another high-finance position somewhere, and…well, it wouldn't be any fun moving to Gabriel Bend and doing this without you."

Lindsey pressed her eyes shut. "My career plans are still up in the air. Who knows what'll happen in three months, or six, or even a year? And I really need you, Jo-Jo. I can't do this without help." Fist clenched, she added, "And I *won't* let my aunt lose the ranch."

More silence. Then, "Let me think and pray about it some more. You do the same, and let's talk again in a few days."

They ended the call with Joella promising she'd have business card designs for Lindsey to choose from in a day or two. But even more heartening was the hope that her friend might actually consider joining forces with her to launch the event venue. If anyone could ensure their success, it was Joella James. And once the venture was firmly established, Lindsey could reassess the direction of her career knowing she'd be leaving the business in good hands and the McClement ranch on solid ground.

And why did looking toward a future that *didn't* include her staying on at the ranch induce such crushing pangs of regret?

Two days later, Joella emailed Lindsey with three strikingly professional business card designs. Audra had ridden out on Skeeter for a quick check of her cattle, but Lindsey couldn't wait to show her. With her laptop tucked under her arm, she grabbed a jacket and scurried out the back door.

Intending to drive the Mule to look for Audra, she was halfway to the shed when she glimpsed Spencer coming out of the barn. She stopped and waved. "How are the horses this morning?"

"Better every day." Striding her way, he cast her

computer a skeptical glance. "Too much time cooped up inside?"

"Now that you mention it, I haven't been away from the desk much lately." She shrugged. "I was actually heading out to find Audra. My friend who did your website emailed me some great business card ideas for our event venue."

"Can I see?"

"Sure. An objective opinion would be great." Back-tracking to the porch steps, she plopped down. When Spencer joined her, she flipped open her computer, then scrolled slowly through the images.

"Go back to the second one." As Spencer studied the screen, his shoulder brushed hers.

She tried to ignore the tremor racing up her spine. "You like the river graphic on the side?" It was pretty, and in some ways did resemble views of the ranch, but the watermark indicated it was a stock photo Joella had found online.

He shifted to tug his phone from his jeans pocket. "Maybe..." he began, thumbing through photos, "she could use this one instead."

A photograph of the river overlook filled the screen. Taken when the trees were just leafing out in spring-time, the image popped with color—blue sky, reddish-brown earth, myriad shades of green.

Lindsey drew a silent breath. "You took this pic-ture? When?"

"Last March, I think." He winced. "I, uh, kind of snuck over one day when I needed a break from Tito's harangues."

"Oh, Spencer, you didn't have to *sneak*. Audra wouldn't have cared at all."

"I know. But at the time, I didn't feel like explaining. Also, your uncle had gotten sick again around then, and I didn't want to bother anyone." He cleared his throat. "So, think your friend could work with this picture?"

"I'm sure she could. Can you AirDrop it to my computer?"

His brows quirked. "That's a thing?"

With a quick shake of her head, she held out her hand for his phone, which was a surprisingly newer model considering his lack of tech savvy. She touched an icon at the bottom of the photo, then selected the AirDrop function. Her computer appeared in the "tap to share" window, and immediately after she touched the icon, the photo popped up in a tiny notification on her computer screen.

"Voilà!" She returned Spencer's phone.

He snorted. "Show-off."

She was already typing a quick email to Joella to go along with the photo. "This is perfect, Spencer. I know Audra will love it, too." And if Joella got right back to her with the changes, she might have time yet today to deliver the design to the printer in town. She'd already called for a quote and was told the cards could be ready early next week.

At the thought of another outlay of cash, she bit back a sigh. But it was the same old story of having to spend money to make money.

Spencer pushed upward. "I should get going."

"Hey, any chance you could spare some time over the next couple of days?" She beamed him a hopeful smile. "Mom and Stan insisted on buying paint for the chapel, and the weather's supposed to be even nicer tomorrow, so I was going to get started."

Pivoting to face her, he narrowed one eye in a doubt-ful grimace. "You're planning to celebrate New Year's Eve painting an old building?"

"Haven't had any better offers. Anyway," she went on, rising to her feet, "the sooner we get the chapel fixed up, the sooner we can hope for some wedding bookings."

"I can wield a paintbrush as good as anyone. Count me in—on one condition." Hope in his gaze, he added, "Let me take you out for dinner tomorrow night?"

Her heart jumped sideways, and she couldn't help a quick glance toward the Navarro ranch. "Is that a good idea?"

"I don't know," he said. "And frankly, I couldn't care less."

Chapter Ten

Wearing his best black jeans, a blue checked shirt and a leather vest, Spencer peeked into the den, where his parents sat watching the evening news.

Mom blinked twice and let out a low whistle. "*¡Qué guapo!* This can't be my same son who walked in the door earlier covered in paint from head to toe."

After spending most of New Year's Eve day helping Lindsey coat the chapel exterior in pristine white, Spencer had taken nearly an hour to scrub the paint off his hands and out of his hair. Moving closer to his mother, he turned his head from side to side. "Did I miss any spots?"

Mom donned her reading glasses for a closer look. "Don't think so. Want to take my car tonight? It's more presentable than your dirty old truck."

"I'm sure Lindsey would appreciate it. Thanks." Spencer was also thankful Tito had retired early to his bedroom so he wouldn't ask questions about where Spencer was going tonight. Or with whom.

Spencer's father jerked his head in the direction of

the McClement ranch. "They haven't put aside the idea of an event venue?"

"No, they haven't. But there's no reason it should affect us."

"I hope you're right." Dad reached for the remote to turn up the TV volume. "Go, enjoy your dinner," he said, flicking a hand toward the door. "However, it would be wise not to mention this date to your grandfather."

Spencer didn't have to be told twice.

On the other hand, he liked thinking of this evening as his first real date with Lindsey. He'd like it even better if he weren't constantly walking a tightrope between family loyalty and a relationship with the woman who'd claimed his heart when they were teenagers.

Wedging his long frame behind the wheel of his mother's electric-blue Hyundai, he felt weird sitting so low to the ground. But the well-maintained compact sedan sure smelled better than the inside of his truck, which would make it a whole lot easier to enjoy the spicy floral scent of Lindsey's perfume.

With his thoughts rushing ahead to the evening out he'd long ago given up hope he'd have, he turned up the McClement driveway. Dusk had fallen, and he braked abruptly when his headlights swept across an older model hatchback parked in front of the house. The car bore an Oklahoma license plate. Neither Lindsey nor Audra had mentioned expecting more visitors over the holidays, though. Who could—

Then he remembered Lindsey's father had moved to Oklahoma after the divorce. If he'd shown up out of the blue, it could only be bad news.

He pulled up behind the car and shut off the engine, then sat there for a long moment trying to decide whether to go knock on the door or call Lindsey from his cell phone. More than anything, he needed to be sure she was okay.

Then the front door flew open, and Lindsey shoved a thickset, graying man onto the porch. "Leave—now!" Her voice was rough with emotion. "We're doing fine without you, and I won't listen to one more word about selling."

The man was definitely Lindsey's father, though looking much older than Spencer's memories of him. He stumbled forward, then turned back with a scowl. "Have it your way. But eventually, you'll *have* to hear me out. Either that, or deal with my lawyer. Because this isn't over by a long shot."

Owen McClement stomped down the porch steps, halting when he noticed the vehicle parked behind his. He looked from Spencer to Lindsey, still standing in the doorway, before clamping his jaw shut and climbing into his car. The engine roared to life, and he circled around and sped down the drive.

Spencer didn't waste another second debating his next move. He threw open the car door and untangled himself from behind the wheel. By the time he made it to the porch, Lindsey was shaking with rage.

"Hey…hey," he murmured, reaching out to her. "It's okay, Linds. He's gone."

Audra came up beside her and squeezed her shoulders. "Lindsey, calm down. You can't let him get to you like this."

"Why did he even come here? What gives him the right?" Then, as if noticing Spencer for the first time, she cast him a regretful frown. "Oh, no—our plans. I'm not even…" Shifting on bare feet, she looked around distractedly.

"Don't worry about it. You're shivering. Let's get you inside."

Moving into the entryway, he kicked the door closed behind them. Audra excused herself to get Lindsey a glass of water. The woman seemed far less disturbed by her brother's arrival than Lindsey. If anything, Audra appeared…undaunted.

Spencer guided Lindsey to the living room sofa, then sat down next to her. "What happened, Linds? When did he show up?"

"I was getting dressed for tonight." She plucked at her calf-length Southwestern-print skirt. "I heard the car, then Audra telling him he couldn't stay, but he insisted we had to talk."

Audra returned with a water glass. "Here you go, honey." While Lindsey sipped, Audra went on, "Owen's throwing his weight around, still trying to convince me to sell the ranch. I told him Lindsey has a plan and we need to give her a little more time."

"And that's when he started in with the legal threats." Lindsey set the glass on an end table. "After which, I blew my cool and threw him out."

"So I noticed." Spencer wished he'd come over ten minutes sooner so he could have personally booted the slimeball out on his rear.

"Please, kids." Leaning forward, Audra clasped Lindsey's hand. "Don't let him ruin your evening."

"Your aunt's right," Spencer said, shifting closer. "You're stronger than he is, Linds. Don't give him that kind of power."

Lindsey shook her head. "I know, and I'm sorry, but

I don't feel much like celebrating anymore." She looked shyly up at him. "Would you stay, though? Please."

Eyes locked with hers, Spencer arched a brow. "Just try getting rid of me. I don't scare off nearly as easily as your dad."

Silently, Audra slipped from the room. Once they were alone, Lindsey cast him a wry smile. "What is it about you, Spencer Navarro? For some crazy reason, being around you makes me feel…less worried. More hopeful." Her glance swept the corners of the room as if she were searching for words. She returned her focus to him. "More grounded."

Her tender expression made his chest ache. Of all the times for words to fail him, when there was so much he wished he could say to her. "Linds…"

"You don't have to say anything. Your being here is enough."

His hand found hers. "There's nowhere else I'd rather be."

It wasn't the fancy New Year's Eve date Lindsey had been anticipating, but in many ways it was so much better. Spencer really did have a calming effect on her, so after the upsetting and unexpected visit from her father, spending a quiet evening at home with Spencer was exactly what she needed. Leaving him to choose something from among Audra's collection of favorite movies on DVD, she went upstairs and changed into a sweatshirt, faded jeans and fleecy slipper socks.

A few minutes later, while Lindsey popped a frozen pizza into the oven, Spencer pried the cap off a chilled bottle of sparkling cider and filled three glasses. Together with Audra, they toasted the new year. When the pizza was ready, Audra shooed Lindsey and Spencer to the living room with their plates and drinks after insisting she'd eat in the kitchen then make it an early night.

Lindsey fully intended to check later to see how much of the pizza her aunt had actually consumed. She'd been eating noticeably better over the last few weeks, looking not quite so gaunt, her clothes fitting more snugly. But after Dad showed up with his demands and threats, Lindsey only hoped Audra was as unruffled as she appeared.

When the movie ended just before eleven, Lindsey tuned the TV to a channel showing the celebration in Times Square, where it was already almost midnight. As the countdown to the ball drop began, she became acutely aware of Spencer's nearness. They'd been sharing the sofa in comfortable companionship for the past couple of hours, but now Lindsey's pulse hammered with the possibility of the time-honored New Year's kiss. The last time she'd been kissed by any man had been at a New Year's Eve party three years ago. She'd been dating a guy from work, and they'd attended a gathering hosted by friends. The midnight kiss had been a surprise and not entirely welcome since she'd already decided their relationship couldn't go anywhere.

It was only tonight that she realized why. All these years, she'd been subconsciously holding every man she dated to the standard of Spencer Navarro, the good and honorable man she'd always known he'd grow up to become. Kind. Compassionate. A steadfast friend through the best and worst of circumstances.

The kind of man she hoped one day to spend the rest of her life with.

Five...four...three...

Spencer's arm brushed hers, the tension in his muscles palpable.

Two...

Breath quickening, she moved her hand closer to his until their pinkies were touching.

One!

The Times Square crowd broke into joyous shouts, and the panning cameras zoomed in on one kissing couple after another.

Lindsey held her breath, willing Spencer to turn toward her. Slowly, he did, his dusky brown eyes filled with longing and a silent question. She leaned ever so slightly toward him. His Adam's apple working, he shifted sideways and stretched one arm around her shoulders. He lowered his gaze to her lips, and she held herself utterly still for his tender and all-too-brief kiss.

"Happy New Year."

"Happy New Year." Her words came out on a contented sigh.

He shifted again, drawing both her hands into his. "Whatever this year brings, I want you to know—" He inhaled a quick breath. "I hope you know how much I care."

She ran her thumbs across his knuckles, the hands of a hardworking man both strong and gentle. "Being with you these past few weeks, knowing I have your friendship and support... It means more than you'll ever know."

Spencer's voice roughened. "I want to be more than your friend, Lindsey."

"I... I want that, too. Always have." She searched his face, seeing the same doubts there that crowded her own thoughts. "But a McClement and a Navarro—is it even possible?"

"I don't know. I hope so." A darker look replaced his brief glimmer of optimism. He stood abruptly. "It's probably best if I go now."

Loath for him to leave with so much left unspoken, she followed him to the door. "See you tomorrow?"

"I'm always around." He snatched his black Stetson from the coat tree in the entry hall.

"Thanks again for all the painting help today. I can't believe how much we got done."

"It looks good." He studied his hat brim. "Everything around the place is looking really good. You'll be ready for business in no time."

An edge of disappointment had crept into his tone. Or was it worry? "Are you having second thoughts that I can pull this off?"

"No. I'm just…" Opening the door, he gave his head a quick shake. "It's nothing, really."

"Why don't I believe you?"

His gaze drifted toward something in the distant darkness. Far away, in the direction of town, a faintly pulsating glow lit the horizon, accompanied by the dull *whump* of exploding fireworks. "I care too much to see you get hurt, that's all."

She crossed her arms. "There you go again, talking like you know something I don't."

When he didn't immediately deny it, she grew even more suspicious.

"Spencer?"

He stepped onto the porch, then pivoted to face her, the intensity of his stare making her stomach churn. "Between your father and my grandfather, all I'm saying is…" One hand reaching up to cradle her cheek, he brushed his lips across her forehead. "Watch your back."

As he strode to his car, she touched her face where his fingertips had rested and imagined she could still feel the warmth. She had every reason to take his warning seriously, so why did she have the nagging feeling he was deflecting—that there was another, more personal reason behind his abrupt departure?

When her aunt sidled up next to her, she startled. "I thought you'd be sound asleep by now."

"My mind won't shut down," Audra said with a yawn. "Been praying and reading my Bible and was on my way to the kitchen for a glass of milk when I saw Spencer leave." She wrapped an arm around Lindsey's waist. "Did you have a nice evening after all?"

"We did." Lindsey nudged the front door shut and twisted the lock. Odd how she rarely concerned herself with locked doors and windows out here in the country… until Dad had shown up. Stifling her own yawn, she suspected that even as tired as she was, sleep would be long in coming for her as well. "Think I'll join you for that glass of milk."

On a working horse ranch, one day was pretty much the same as the next, and Spencer and his father worked as hard as the hired hands, even more so on holidays. "We're the ones with skin in the game," Dad always said, "so if we expect our employees' loyalty the rest of the year, we carry the load so they can take time off to celebrate with their families."

Skin in the game. Exactly what Lindsey's father didn't have since he'd checked out on his family. Early on New Year's morning, as Spencer mucked his rescue horses' stalls in Audra's barn, the encounter with Owen Mc-Clement yesterday played heavily on his mind. He hadn't spoken a word to the man, but Lindsey's reaction—and her mood for the rest of the evening—had said plenty.

For a couple of hours, though, munching on pizza and chuckling over the romantic comedy DVD he'd selected because he thought Lindsey would enjoy it, he could almost imagine they were a normal couple on a stay-at-home date. No concerns about ranch foreclosure sales. No stressing over equine rescue fundraising.

No feuding relatives conspiring to keep them apart.

Spencer couldn't shake the sense that there was something off about the timing of Owen McClement showing up when he had. Why now, when he'd had months to try convincing Audra to sell?

And Tito's mysterious business in town—what was that about? Spencer had no doubt his grandfather was still working on some scheme to position himself to snatch the McClement ranch if Lindsey's efforts failed.

"Hey." Lindsey's lazy greeting caught him by surprise. He swung around to see her resting her arms on the open stall gate.

"Hey, yourself." His breath caught at the sight of her—hair in a lopsided ponytail, faded jeans, the tails of a wrinkled flannel shirt peeking out from beneath an oversize gray sweater. "Thought maybe you'd sleep in today."

"Couldn't. Literally." Lips mashed into a thoughtful pout, she glanced away.

Oh, how he'd love to kiss away her worries and make everything all right.

He returned to plying his pitchfork. "Had a little trouble sleeping myself."

For the next few minutes, Lindsey silently watched him work, occasionally dodging a misaimed forkful of shavings on its way to the wheelbarrow. When he finished with the stalls, she walked out with him to empty the soiled shavings into the collection bin. All the while, he had the feeling she wanted to talk about something but didn't know how.

Last night's kiss, perhaps? Because he sure hadn't stopped thinking about it.

When she still hadn't said anything by the time he was ready to head home, he paused outside the barn. Hands on hips, he faced her. "Are we okay?"

Her brows shot up. "Of course. Why would you even ask?"

"Because until now, you'd said exactly three words to me this morning, and then you dogged my every step like you had plenty more on your mind."

Hands jammed into her jeans pockets, she heaved an exaggerated shrug. "Guess I wanted to be sure *you* thought we were okay. After last night, I mean. Because you left in kind of a hurry, and I thought maybe you were sorry—"

"About kissing you? Never." Spencer's throat thickened with emotion. "The only thing I'm sorry about is how the trouble between our families is messing with our lives. Our futures. And I want to protect you from that, but I'm not sure I can."

"I don't expect you to. But maybe…" Her gaze drifted toward the Navarro ranch. "Maybe it's time we stopped giving this feud so much control."

"Ignoring it won't make it go away." Not while Tito was alive, anyway.

Spencer immediately berated himself for the direction of his thoughts. He'd never wish his grandfather gone. He only wanted the man to release his bitterness to God and find contentment in what he had, before it was too late.

"You're giving me that look again." Lindsey skewered him with her pointed stare.

He flinched. "What look?"

"The one you get when you're about to cut the conversation short."

Wow, she knew him almost better than he knew himself. He had no reply.

"Fine." Hands raised, she retreated. "You have work to do and so do I."

"Linds—"

"No rest for the weary, and all that. Thought I'd get started on the inside of the chapel today." Her fake cheeriness wasn't fooling him. "See you around?"

"I'll try to come over later and help."

"Sure, if you have time." Tossing him a jaunty wave, she pivoted on the toe of her sneaker and strode toward one of the utility buildings.

Great. Once—just once—couldn't he trade his crummy communication skills for his twin brother's silver-tongued charm? *I'm in love with you, Lindsey,* he'd say, *and I'm scared to death that once you've saved your family's ranch, I'll lose you. And I don't think I'd survive the heartbreak.*

Chapter Eleven

After two days of sweeping debris, scrubbing grime off windows and sanding rough spots from the chapel benches, Lindsey stood in the center of the small space and assessed her progress. A few more repairs had to be made, but the building was beginning to look functional again.

"Looks pretty good," Audra said, peering in through the open door. "Wish you'd let me help."

"You have plenty to do with the horses and cattle every morning. I'm the one who should be helping you instead of..." Lindsey flicked a limp strand of hair off her forehead. There she went with the self-doubts again. Her emotions ricocheted all over the place lately, so much so that she'd turned away Spencer's latest offers to lend a hand with the chapel. Considering he played a huge part in her current state of confusion, she'd tactfully suggested he'd be of more use tidying up around the barn and other outbuildings.

He hadn't complained, but she could tell from his expression that she'd disappointed him. It was better this way, though. They were naive to think anything could come of these feelings neither of them seemed able to open up about.

Audra wandered inside and plopped onto the end of a bench. "What's on your mind, honey? You've been awfully subdued since…"

"Since Dad showed up uninvited?" Lindsey took the bench across from her aunt. "You'd tell me if you heard from him again, right?"

"Of course I would." Audra's focus wandered, then returned to Lindsey. "I can handle his bluster and threats. I'm not sure you can."

"I don't understand him. Much less why he thinks he should have any say in what you do with the ranch."

Tires on gravel drew their attention. Audra rose and looked out toward the driveway. Shoulders stiffening, she cast Lindsey a meaningful frown. "Keep your cool this time, and maybe you can ask him yourself."

Lindsey clutched her roiling stomach as she edged to the door. "He's back?"

"I won't have a repeat of the other night, do you understand?" Audra wrapped her fingers around Lindsey's forearm and gave a light squeeze. "We'll handle this calmly and respectfully." She closed her eyes briefly. "And prayerfully. God is in control, honey. Never forget that."

Lindsey inhaled a shaky breath before following her aunt toward the front of the house. *Calmly and respectfully?* Those qualities would definitely require divine intervention where her father was concerned.

When they reached the front porch, she found her father pacing and fuming. He swung around, his gaze connecting with Lindsey's, and for a fleeting moment she thought she sensed regret. He quickly covered it with the swipe of a hand down his face. "There you are."

"This is a ranch," Lindsey stated. "We've been working."

Audra eased in front of her, a subtle message to rein in her emotions. "Come inside and I'll put on a pot of coffee. Then we can talk."

Her aunt's cordial tone settled Lindsey's dad. His stiff posture relaxing slightly, he moved aside to let Audra lead the way. Stalling, Lindsey motioned him through the door ahead of her. She'd take advantage of every spare moment to prepare herself for another showdown.

In the kitchen, Audra had pushed the start button on the coffee maker. "Have a seat, Owen. Care for a slice of pumpkin bread with your coffee?"

"Uh, sure." He took a chair at the far end of the table.

Lindsey busied herself getting plates, forks and napkins while Audra cut three hearty slices from the loaf. She'd been baking again yesterday, the aroma filling the house and tempting Lindsey's taste buds. Today, though, she doubted she could choke down a single morsel.

With the coffee poured and the pumpkin bread served, Audra chose the chair nearest her brother, sparing Lindsey, who seated herself at the opposite end of the table, then did her best not to look directly at her father.

No one said anything for several tense moments while nibbling—or pretending to, anyway—on their pumpkin bread.

Then Lindsey's father nudged his plate aside and leaned his elbows on his knees. "Look, I'm not trying to be unreasonable here. Just realistic."

A caustic remark begged for release from Lindsey's lips, but Audra silenced her with a light tap on her hand. "I respect your point of view, Owen. I also know this ranch never held the same meaning for you that it has for me. Perhaps I'm not being completely realistic in wanting to hold on to it. But for you to be so insistent about selling… I can't help but think your only interest is the money."

"I admit, that's part of it. My…my stepkids…" He slid his glance toward Lindsey, then looked away. "DeeDee and I got married last month, and, well, families are expensive."

Lindsey trembled with the effort required to hold her tongue. She didn't know how much more of this she could take.

He whipped a folded paper from his breast pocket and slapped it open in front of Audra. "I tried to talk to you about this the other night. It's a more than fair offer on the property, enough to pay off the debts and set us up real nice for the foreseeable future."

Snatching the page, Lindsey scanned the official-looking document. "Where'd you get this?"

"An Austin real estate broker emailed it to me last week." His mouth twisted in a smug smile. "Guess the prospective buyer figured I'd be more open to negotiating than my stubborn sister."

"You still can't make a deal without Audra's agreement," Lindsey muttered while searching for the line naming the buyer. "Ah, another corporation with a suspiciously obscure name."

"Doesn't matter who the offer's from. It's legit. Come on, sis, why wouldn't you jump at the chance to get this albatross off your neck?"

"Albatross?" Lindsey flew from her chair.

"Honey, sit down." Aggravatingly calm, Audra waited until Lindsey had complied, then shifted to face her brother. "What's really going on here, Owen? Why do you despise this ranch so much?"

"I don't." He swallowed hard, his glance shifting uneasily between Audra and Lindsey before he looked directly toward the Navarro ranch. "It's *them* I despise. Every last high-handed, coldhearted one of them."

This was too much. And completely irrational. "How can you lump them all together like that?" Lindsey burst out, then bit her lip as she recalled doing pretty much the same thing with Spencer only a few weeks ago. She forced a measure of calm into her tone. "The feud was between Grandpa and Arturo. You can't possibly think all the Navarros are out to get you personally."

"Oh, no?" His cold stare held hers. He clenched his jaw so tightly that it quivered. "There's a lot you don't know, Lindsey. Stuff that should make you want to stay as far away from that family as you can—"

He cut himself off suddenly. As if he'd read her mind—or more likely the pained look in her expression—he continued, "I'm too late, aren't I? You're getting involved with one of those Navarro boys." He gave his head a disgusted shake. "You're asking for trouble, Lindsey. Play with fire and you'll get burned..." His tone fell to a murmur. "Like I did."

While Lindsey tried to make sense of his statement, Audra studied her brother, a look of comprehension widening her eyes. "I was too young then to realize... You were in love with Alicia, weren't you?"

Nodding, he sat back with a thud. "And because of it, the Navarros ruined both our lives."

Lindsey gulped for air as if someone had cut off her oxygen supply. "So Mom was your consolation prize? Did you ever even love her?"

"Linds, don't." He stretched his hand toward her across the table, but she recoiled. "I admit, I was an angry, hurting mess after Arturo refused to let us get married. I hated my father, too, for not standing up for us. So I packed and left. Got a job in West Texas working oil rigs. Met your mom and tried to forget all about Alicia Navarro."

"But you couldn't," Lindsey said flatly. "That's why you and Mom fought so much, isn't it? Why you gave up on us and walked out."

His silence was the only confirmation she needed.

She rose and emptied her cold coffee into the sink. Standing before the window, she looked beyond the ugly barbed-wire fence as Spencer led a saddled horse toward the arena. Even with all her doubts and misgivings, her heart lifted at the sight of him. This feud must not win.

Whirling around, she faced her father. "I'm sorry for you. Sorry you let a stubborn old man dictate your happiness. Even sorrier you took out your resentment on Mom and me. But I'm not going to repeat your mistakes, and I'm not going to let you force your sister to give up the ranch she's more than earned the right to keep. If it means me holding down three jobs so I can help Audra raise the money to buy you out, I'll do it. Name your price."

"Lindsey—" Teary-eyed, Audra reached out to her.

She crossed the kitchen to stand behind her aunt's chair. Resting her hands on Audra's shoulders, she hiked her chin. "I'm serious, Dad. Whatever it takes, the ranch is staying in the family."

He stared at her for a long, tense moment, then slowly stood. Retrieving the offer to purchase, he ripped it into four ragged pieces and tossed it in the center of the table. "Fine, Lindsey. If you want it that badly, it's yours. First thing Monday, I'll have my lawyer legally transfer my share of the ranch to you. Consider it an early start on your inheritance. If you want to dig your own grave trying to save this place, more power to you."

Lindsey's jaw dropped. Had she heard him right? "Dad…"

Halfway to the entry hall, he halted without turning around. "And just so you know, it was never about the money."

The front door slammed behind him.

The roar of an engine followed by the squeal of tires on pavement snapped Spencer's head up and startled his horse. "Easy, boy. You're fine."

The animal settled, and Spencer peered toward the road to see the same beat-up hatchback driving away that had been parked in front of Audra's house on New Year's Eve. Lindsey's dad again?

Spencer's grandfather, who had been observing this training ride from the bleacher seats at the end of the arena, slapped his thigh. "You see what is happening? If those people are allowed to commercialize their property, such disturbances will only get worse. Who knows what kind of riffraff their outrageous event venue will attract?"

"*Those people* are our neighbors, Tito." Spencer

wouldn't state the obvious—that the Navarro quarter horse ranch was also a commercial operation.

Concerned for Lindsey, he struggled to keep the high-strung horse steady while he tugged out his phone and typed a quick text. U OK?

"You need to stop spending so much time over there," his grandfather ranted on. "If you're determined to pursue your rescue program, we can build you a barn right here, far enough away from our horses so as not to be a concern."

How many times had Spencer proposed that idea and been shot down? It would be an unjustifiable expense, the rescues already took up too much of Spencer's time, and so on and so on. Now, it seemed his grandfather was grasping at anything to cut off all association between the Navarros and McClements.

He checked his phone. No reply yet. Minutes ticked by, and all he could do was continue putting the horse through its paces. This smart, smooth-moving gelding would go to a cattle rancher in Juniper Bluff who needed a reliable cutting horse for working his herd.

Either because Spencer refused to engage in argument or because he'd satisfied his grandfather's expectations about the gelding's training, the old man eventually clambered down from the bleachers and returned to the house. Tito was definitely moving more slowly these days.

As he finished up the ride, his phone vibrated. Finally, Lindsey replied with a double thumbs-up and a message. Crazy day. Tell you all about it later.

Relieved, and more than a little curious, Spencer untacked the horse and brushed him down, then returned him to the pasture. He'd scheduled two more training rides for the afternoon, and by the time he'd completed them, the winter sun was sinking behind the hills. Hungry and exhausted, he trudged toward the back porch.

As he pulled open the screen door, loud voices reached him from the kitchen. It sounded like Tito was on another tear about something. More than likely, it involved the McClement ranch.

At that moment, his mother burst onto the porch. The door to the kitchen slammed behind her. Seeing Spencer, she drew up short. "You don't want to go in there right now."

He didn't like the angry glint in Mom's eyes. "Why? What's Tito carrying on about?"

"I can't believe he's done this, that he'd stoop so low—"

"Mom, *what*?"

She blew out a ragged breath. "Arturo and his lawyer created some kind of anonymous legal entity for trying to buy the McClement ranch. Except they completely bypassed Audra and were trying to negotiate with her brother."

"Lindsey's dad?" Spencer yanked off his hat and raked stiff fingers through his hair. No wonder Owen McClement had shown up out of the blue. "Of all the backstabbing—"

"Apparently, the offer got nowhere. Audra's still refusing to sell, and Owen couldn't change her mind."

Which would explain why Owen had sped off earlier.

Spencer slapped his hat back on his head. Somehow, he felt responsible, even if none of this was his doing. "I need to go see Lindsey."

Mom gripped his arm. "Be careful, son. If I hadn't walked in on your grandfather talking to his lawyer, we'd all still be in the dark about this. No one was supposed to know. Not even your dad."

"Then having his scheme exposed will serve Tito right." With a quick glance of apology to his mother, Spencer tugged free of her hand and marched out.

Two minutes later, he was rapping on Audra's front door.

She answered with a surprised smile. "Spencer. Come on in."

She looked a lot cheerier than he would have expected, all things considered. His news would likely wipe that smile right off her face. "I don't want to interrupt dinner."

"We're finished." Audra opened the door wider. "Lindsey's starting a pot of decaf. Will you have some?"

"No, thanks." Hat tucked against his chest, he entered the foyer. "I, uh, have something I need to tell you. Tell you both."

Audra's brow creased. She motioned him toward the kitchen. "Lindsey? We have company."

"Please tell me it isn't—" Her face brightened the moment she saw Spencer. "Oh, hi. I've been waiting all day to tell you what happened."

"Spencer says he has news, too," Audra said, concern in her tone. "Maybe we should let him go first."

With both Audra and Lindsey staring at him, he didn't know how to begin. He set his hat on the table and hauled in a steadying breath. "My grandfather has done something."

The women shared a meaning-fraught glance before Lindsey spoke. "Would this have anything to do with a suspicious corporation wanting to buy our ranch?"

He swallowed hard. "I'm so sorry. Nobody in the

family knew he was doing this. I only found out a few minutes ago."

"It's all right, Spencer." Lindsey turned to the coffeepot and filled two mugs. She handed one to Spencer before seating herself at the table.

He frowned at the coffee he hadn't asked for and didn't think he could choke down. *Why wasn't she more upset?*

Audra poured some decaf for herself. Mug in hand, she passed behind Lindsey and patted her on the shoulder. "Think I'll go in the living room so y'all can talk between yourselves."

As Audra disappeared around the corner, he looked back at Lindsey. "I know your aunt refused the offer, but still—realizing my grandfather would do such a thing—"

"It's not your fault, Spencer. You don't have to apologize for him." Looking like the cat who'd swallowed the canary, Lindsey sipped her coffee. "Are you ready to hear my news now?"

He gingerly set down his mug and lowered himself into a chair. "Maybe you'd better tell me quick, because I am way beyond confused right now."

She sat up a little straighter. "As of Monday morning, my father will no longer be half owner of the McClement ranch."

"I don't understand."

"When Dad couldn't talk Audra into accepting the offer, he was livid. Mad enough," she added smugly, "to wash his hands completely of the ranch and sign his share over to me. His attorney already phoned me to get the specifics for drawing up the papers so he can have them ready for signatures by Monday morning."

Spencer gave his head a quick shake. "Then you…"

"That's right. Audra and I will be co-owners, and my dad will be out of the picture." Even as she spoke the words, her confident expression faltered. "It's still sinking in exactly what this will mean for the ranch." She glanced away, her lower lip trembling. "For me. For my future."

Spencer couldn't help wondering the same thing. His hand crept across the table, closer and closer to where hers rested near her coffee mug. Their fingers grazed. "I know what I'd like it to mean."

Her hand slipped into his. "All this time, I thought I was trying to save the ranch for Audra's sake. But now I realize it's more than that. Always has been." She lifted those gorgeous brown eyes to meet his gaze. "Every summer I spent here as a kid, every ounce of effort I've put into this place over the past few weeks—it's because no place I've ever lived has felt more like I belonged."

Spencer's heart hammered the backside of his breastbone. "So…you're staying?"

"Yes, I'm staying." A smile spread across Lindsey's face, as if she'd only this moment admitted it to herself. "This ranch is my home now, and I'm not going anywhere."

Waves of relief surged over him, along with the ridiculous hope that the day would finally come when they could put the Navarro-McClement feud behind them once and for all. He reached for his Stetson and absently pinched the crown. "It's true I thought for a while that selling the ranch would be the best thing for Audra. My grandfather even had me convinced that when the ranches were divided, your grandfather somehow cheated him out of the best acreage."

"My grandfather was not a cheat," Lindsey stated. "He would never—"

"I believe you. I also believe there are two sides to this feud and that we may never know the whole story."

"One thing I found out today…" Lindsey's tone grew serious. "You and I aren't the only couple our families have tried to keep apart."

She'd begun to think of them as a couple? That alone was reason to hope. There was someone else, though? "Who?"

She tipped her coffee mug to swirl the contents, then set it back down with a thunk. "Did you know that my father and your aunt Alicia were once in love?"

Spencer stared at her in shock. "You're kidding."

"Dad claims it's why he could never fully commit to Mom. Why they fought so much." A tear pooled beneath her eye. "Why he left us."

"Aw, Linds." Without a second thought, he rose and drew her into a hug. "I had no idea. I'm so sorry."

She tucked her arms around his waist. "I know. It's crazy."

Holding her, all he wanted was to protect her from every hurtful thing their families had ever done or might do to each other. To pretend he wasn't a Navarro and that she wasn't a McClement. That they could blink their eyes twice and wake up in a world where love triumphed over greed and deceit and life made sense again.

Chapter Twelve

Sitting in church with her aunt on Sunday morning, Lindsey struggled to keep her thoughts centered on the readings and message. Her mind kept replaying those moments in Spencer's arms last night, his tender kiss before he said he needed to get home and clear up a few things with his father and grandfather.

She'd urged him not to confront them—not yet, at least. As often as he'd encouraged her to trust God and go forward in faith, she couldn't bear it if his grand-father's destructive choices caused him to lose faith. "We both need to pray about how to handle this," she'd told him. He'd seemed both surprised and grateful to hear her speak those words.

She'd been a little surprised herself. God had cer-tainly been working on her heart these past few weeks, and she wished she could have attended worship with Spencer this morning so they could come before God united in prayer. But the Navarros and McClements hadn't belonged to the same church since the ranch was divided all those years ago. If Lindsey and Spencer did break free from their pasts and plan a future together, then would be the time for them to look for a new church home, where they could worship as a couple without the shadow of the feud continually hanging over them.

With still so much she wanted to do before Wednesday, when Jenny Thomas and her fiancé had scheduled their photographer at the ranch, Lindsey got straight to work that afternoon. During one of her horseback rides with Audra to tend the cattle, she'd come upon an ancient live oak she remembered climbing on as a kid. The tree had grown even taller, its small, elongated leaves still green this time of year and the branches stretching wide to form a graceful canopy. Lindsey could easily picture the bride-to-be and her handsome fiancé embracing beneath the boughs.

It would be advantageous to have various locations around the ranch that she could suggest for photography settings. Loading tools into the back of the Mule, she planned to do some scouting on her way out to clean up around the oak tree.

Amazing how her attitude had changed since yesterday after her father's sudden decision to sign over his share of the ranch. It had been one thing to cosign a consolidation loan to help Audra dig out from under her debts. Going forward, they'd be equal partners in any ranching decisions, and the thought both terrified and exhilarated her.

At least they shared a common goal—to keep the ranch in the family and make it profitable again. Combining Audra's knowledge of cattle and land management with Lindsey's business sense—and, she hoped, with some event planning and catering assistance from Holly and Joella—how could they fail?

While clearing brush from beneath the oak tree, she

made a mental note to contact her friends again and plant a bug in their ears about the possibility of moving to Gabriel Bend. Holly's little boy would have a blast exploring the ranch, and Austin wasn't that far away for when Davey needed specialty medical care. Getting out of the corporate rat race would be so good for Joella, too. She'd sounded more than a little jaded the last time Lindsey had talked to her.

It was nearing five o'clock by the time she finished and headed back. On her way to the house after putting her tools away, she glimpsed Spencer walking Cinnamon and Ash into the barn for the night.

"Hi," she called, hurrying over. "Can I help?"

He eyed her up and down as he passed her Cinnamon's lead rope. "Looks like you've already been hard at work this afternoon."

"Hmm, not sure how to take that." Grinning, she flicked a tangled strand off her forehead.

Once the horses were secured in their stalls with fresh feed and water, Lindsey's fatigue caught up with her. She plopped onto a tack trunk, leaned back and stretched out both legs.

Spencer sat down beside her and drew her hand into his lap, weaving his fingers through hers. "Still excited to be half owner of the McClement ranch?"

"I am. I'll be even more excited when the paperwork is filed to make it official."

"You don't think your dad will change his mind, do you?"

She shrugged. "It's possible, I guess. But I get the feeling Dad's ready to wash his hands of it all." Tilting her head so she could read Spencer's expression, she asked, "How about you? Any more fallout at your house since yesterday?"

"I've purposely kept my distance from Tito." He grimaced. "Don't trust myself not to let him have it with both barrels."

"I'm so sorry, Spencer. I hate that all this is coming between you and your family."

His fingers tightened around hers. "Same with you. I felt awful for you the summer your dad left. Makes me sick now to know my grandfather was part of the reason why."

"Don't. We aren't responsible for their choices. Anyway," she said, bumping shoulders with him, "if my father had married your aunt, I wouldn't be me."

He gave a half-hearted chuckle. "Or worse, you'd be my pesky first cousin."

"Yikes!" She faked a shudder. Then, with a dreamy sigh, she rested her cheek in the hollow of Spencer's chest. "So…despite all the problems our forebears have caused us, guess there's a silver lining after all."

Spencer wanted to believe in silver linings. He wanted to believe what he and Lindsey shared was real and lasting, impervious to any pressure their families might exert. But he couldn't easily shake off what she'd told him about her father and his aunt. It had to be nearly forty years in the past—Aunt Alicia had been married to David Caldwell almost that long—yet Lindsey's father had apparently never released his grudge. Both sets of grandparents likely deserved blame for keeping the couple apart, but with Lindsey's grandparents no longer living, how could Tito continue to allow this feud to destroy more lives?

And even though Spencer had promised Lindsey he'd pray before taking any action, his anger had festered to the point of making his time with God less a two-way conversation than a one-sided rant. For the present, at least, it was easier to avoid his grandfather as much as possible, or else risk the temptation to lash out with all his pent-up accusations and unanswered questions.

The next couple of days kept him busy working with the quarter horses and seeing to his rescues. On Tuesday afternoon the Foxes came to take Cinnamon home. Spencer would miss the sweet little horse, but the joy on Timothy's face helped to ease the goodbye. Lindsey came out as the family was leaving and shed a tear or two as she and Spencer watched the pickup and horse trailer head down the driveway.

Lindsey's hand crept into his. "At least we still have Ash."

"He'll eventually go to a new home, too, you know." Her affection for the horses tugged at his heart. "But don't worry, more are coming. Deputy Miller called this morning to ask if I could foster a couple of older mares a farmer's relinquishing. They're in good health, but he's too broke to keep feeding them."

She pulled a tissue from her pocket and blew her nose. "I used to think I'd like to be a foster parent, but I'm realizing I'm no good at goodbyes."

"Would you want kids of your own…someday?" It was a question best saved for the woman he hoped to marry—and it seemed she was standing right next to him.

"Yeah," she said, her tone turning wistful. "When the time is right, I want to be a mom." Inhaling deeply, she turned in a slow circle. "And what better place to raise kids than right here?" She was obviously still basking in the satisfaction of signing the papers that made her co-owner of the McClement ranch.

He was happy for her but couldn't help wondering what her increased stake in the ranch would mean for the two of them. It hurt to feel so torn inside—his growing feelings for Lindsey pitted against the loyalty he should have for his family heritage.

He roughly cleared his throat. "I should get home. Got plenty more to do while it's still daylight."

"Same here. I have a couple of odd jobs to finish before Jenny and Zach come out with their photographer tomorrow."

"What time are you expecting them?"

"Late afternoon, maybe three thirty or four." Lindsey shrugged. "Supposedly that's when the light's the best."

"Should be nice weather for it. Deputy Miller mentioned bringing the mares over tomorrow, but I'll ask him to come plenty early so we aren't in the way."

"Thanks." Backing up, she tucked her fingers into her jeans pockets. "Well, see you later."

"Yeah. Later."

Funny how they could be so comfortable around each other at times, then go back to the awkwardness. Or was it the lingering shadow of the feud that made everything seem so uncertain?

On his way across the field toward home, he called Deputy Miller and explained the situation with Lindsey. "So if you can be here and gone by three o'clock, I'd appreciate it."

"Got it. Should be able to make it by noon."

That settled, Spencer wrapped up his evening tasks and headed inside to clean up for supper.

In the kitchen, he looked at the table, then at his mother. "Only three places?"

She frowned. "Arturo's in his room. Said he didn't feel like eating."

Not that Spencer minded a less tension-filled supper with only his parents, but this had been happening more and more often. "Has Dad gotten him to see the doctor yet?"

"He's tried, but you know how stubborn your grandfather is." She set a bowl of buttered peas next to the platter of pork chops. "Honestly, the way he's been carrying on about the McClements, I'm surprised he hasn't given himself a heart attack already."

Spencer couldn't disagree, but it only made him sadder about the feud and angrier with Tito for letting it run his life.

The old man seemed to be feeling fine at breakfast the next morning, though, talking a blue streak about "those McClements" and how their event venue plans were sure to wreak havoc for the Navarro horses. Spencer closed his ears to the tirade and didn't stick around any longer than it took to wolf down a bowl of cereal and fill a travel mug with coffee.

The farrier was coming out to trim hooves and replace shoes on several of the horses, a job that would take the better part of the day, and Spencer needed to be on hand to assist. He also hoped the farrier would have time to look at Ash's hooves. The old horse hadn't shown any obvious signs yet, but laminitis remained a concern.

Helping a stable hand move horses back and forth between their pastures and the farrier's trailer, Spencer soon lost track of time. He only realized it was past noon when his mother brought him a sandwich, which he gulped down while watching the farrier file the hoof of one of the less fidgety young fillies.

Sometime later, he became vaguely aware of vehicle sounds and the crunch of tires on gravel next door. Must be about time for the photo shoot. Which meant—

The deputy should have already brought the mares over. Had he missed a call or text? He yanked his cell phone from his pocket only to find a black screen and a dead battery. Guess he'd been too preoccupied last night to put it on the charger.

He'd just brought in another horse and handed off the lead rope to the stable hand. "Be right back. Gotta make a quick call."

On his way to the house, he glimpsed the sheriff's department vehicle and horse trailer turning into the McClement driveway—right behind Jenny Thomas's SUV and trailer. Great. Exactly what he'd hoped to avoid. Nothing to do now except hurry over and hope to unload the two new rescues with as little commotion as possible.

First, though, he needed to let his father know so he could take over with the farrier. He found him in Tito's office. Hanging up the phone, Tito turned with a self-satisfied smirk. Dad stood unmoving, his nostrils flared and jaw clenched. His gaze connected with Spencer's in a look of silent apology.

Belly tensing, Spencer backed away. "What's going on here?"

"You'll know soon enough," Tito said. Still grinning, he strode past Spencer toward the front of the house.

"Dad?"

"I tried, son, but I couldn't talk him out of this. This is still his ranch. He has the final say."

"What did—"

The distant wail of a siren cut short his question. Heart hammering, he spun around and ran to the living room, joining Tito at the front windows. As he watched, a sheriff's car with lights flashing turned up the McClement driveway.

Spencer moved in front of his grandfather. Suspecting he already knew the answer, he looked Tito in the eyes. "What have you done?"

"Lindsey?" Audra's anxious tone echoed off the entryway ceiling. "You'd better come out here."

"Be right there." She grabbed the invoice she'd printed, so proud of how professional it looked with the logo Joella had designed.

Their first official client—exciting! A few minutes ago, Jenny had driven around back with her horse trailer, followed by a silver compact SUV, probably the photographer. Lindsey had intended to be outside to greet them as they drove up, but the printer had jammed and it had taken three tries before it spit out a clean, unwrinkled copy of the invoice.

By then, the livestock deputy had driven up. Lindsey couldn't deal with him now and hoped Spencer was on his way over. What happened to delivering the rescue horses early enough not to interfere with the photo shoot?

Smoothing back a flyaway curl, she found Audra standing in the open front door. "What's going on? Did I hear sirens?"

"Afraid so. Seems we have some unexpected company."

Brow furrowed, Lindsey looked out at the sheriff's department vehicle parked at the base of the porch steps.

A grim-faced deputy emerged and marched up to the porch. He consulted an official-looking paper. "Are you ladies Audra Forrester and Lindsey McClement?"

"Yes, I'm Mrs. Forrester. This is Lindsey, my niece." Arms crossed, Audra stepped forward. "What's this about, please?"

"Ma'am, we've had a complaint resulting in a judge's order for you to cease and desist any and all activities on this property conducted by River Bend Events and Wedding Chapel."

Momentarily speechless, Lindsey wagged her head. They'd barely gotten their business registration filed and hadn't even done any real advertising yet. Who could possibly know—

The Navarros. And who besides Spencer's grandfather had enough clout in this county to sway a judge to issue such an order? If he couldn't persuade Audra to sell outright, he'd do whatever was necessary to push her further into bankruptcy.

A motion at the fence line caught her eye. Spencer had vaulted the barbed wire and was jogging across the field. Breathless, he tromped up to the porch. "Lindsey, I'm sorry," he said between gasps. "I didn't know."

Jenny and Zach appeared from the other direction. "Um, hi," Jenny said. "We were wondering if we could get started?"

Lips parted, Lindsey looked from Jenny to the deputy to Spencer and back again. "I, uh…" She crumpled the invoice in her left fist. "I'm afraid we're going to have to cancel."

Audra pulled herself together enough to give Jenny and her fiancé a more gracious explanation and apology while walking them back to where they'd parked. Before the deputy left, Lindsey vaguely heard him say they could file an appeal, but of course that would take time, not to mention attorney's fees they couldn't spare. Spencer reluctantly excused himself to help unload the rescues, and even though none of this was his fault, she couldn't bring herself to look at him.

Alone on the porch, she sank onto the top step and buried her face in her hands. *Why, God? Just when things seemed to be moving in the right direction, You pull the rug out from under me.*

Hearing vehicles starting up behind the house, she shoved to her feet and hurried inside. From behind the living room curtains, she watched first Jenny's SUV and horse trailer drive away, then the photographer's car. A few minutes later, the livestock deputy left.

Audra came in through the kitchen. Finding Lindsey in a heap of misery on the sofa, she wrapped her in a tender hug. "Oh, sweetie, don't cry. We'll fight this. We'll—"

"How can we? Arturo will only come back at us harder than ever." She lifted her head to cast her aunt a despairing frown. "I'm so, so sorry. I thought I could save the ranch for you—for both of us. I was wrong. I've failed you, and now things are even worse than when I came."

"Don't say that." Audra shifted to grip Lindsey's shoulders. "You could not fail me if you tried. I love you, and I'm so proud of you. And even if God does show us it's time to let this place go, I've told you before, land and cattle will never be more important than family. Wherever God places us, we will survive—and *thrive*."

Lindsey knew her aunt was doing her best to hold on to hope, but right now, those were meaningless words. "I can't even think—"

A knock sounded on the back door.

"I'm sure that's Spencer." Audra rose and started for the kitchen.

Too late and too softly for her aunt to hear, Lindsey murmured, "I don't want to see him." *Ever.*

Then he was standing right in front of her, hat in hand. "Linds—"

"Don't." She lifted both hands, palms outward. "Just...don't." Pushing up from the sofa, she scooted around him and crossed the room, turning her back to him. "I don't know what I was thinking. Your family and mine—there'll never be peace between us, and it was ludicrous for us to hope otherwise."

"You don't mean that. Lindsey, please—"

She silenced him with an upraised hand. "You can stable your rescues here for now. But I'd appreciate it if you'd start looking for another location as soon as possible. It would be a conflict of interest for us to keep—to continue seeing—" She shuddered. "I—I can't keep doing this. Just go."

For long moments, all she heard was the ragged, desperate sound of his breathing. His boot heels thudded softly upon the hardwood floor of the entryway. The front door whispered open...then clicked shut.

Except for the inconsolable throb of a broken heart, utter silence reigned.

Chapter Thirteen

Spencer burst through the back door, startling his mother as she folded clothes in the laundry room. "Where's Dad? I have to talk to him right now."

"He said he'd be working in the barn office. Hey, did you hear those sirens earlier? Any idea what's—"

He didn't give her a chance to finish. Bolting out again, he tore across to the barn. "Dad!"

"Right here, son." Wearing a resigned frown, his father appeared in the office doorway. "What happened with the sheriff?"

"What *happened*? He shut Lindsey down, that's what!" Spencer shoved past his father and sank into one of the leather armchairs in front of the desk. With all the racing back and forth he'd done in the past hour, his lungs felt like their stallion Concho had kicked him in the chest.

Or else this was what it felt like to have his heart crushed by the woman he loved.

His father took the chair next to him and blew out a long, tired sigh. "When your grandfather sets his mind to something, he won't be dissuaded. I know Lindsey is your friend, but—"

"She's more than a friend." His voice shook. He leaned forward, fists pressed into his eye sockets. "Dad, I'm in love with her."

A low moan escaped his father's throat. "I was afraid of this."

Spencer sat up, twisting to look at his father. "Did you know about Lindsey's dad and Aunt Alicia?"

Dad's brief expression of surprise faded to resignation. He nodded. "Alicia was eighteen, and I was only a high school freshman, but I could tell something was going on. I lost count of how many times our parents argued about how to keep them apart. Mama's sister lived in Denver, so as soon as Alicia graduated, they pushed her into moving in with our aunt and attending college there. Owen left not long afterward. I heard he'd found work in the oil fields."

Gazing out the window, Spencer muttered, "Maybe that's what I should do, too."

"You don't mean that." Dad gripped Spencer's forearm hard enough that he flinched.

"Why not? I can no longer live under the same roof with a man who thinks he can manipulate lives like Tito does. I've lost all respect for him." He swung back to glare at his father. "And for you, if you can look me in the eye and honestly tell me you don't see what's wrong with what he's done."

"I never— Spencer, you don't understand."

"No, Dad, I don't, and that's a real problem." He shoved back the chair, stumbling past his father and out the door.

Barely acknowledging his mother as he tore through the kitchen, he stormed to his room and began throwing clothes into a duffel bag.

Seconds later, she stood beside him and yanked a wadded-up T-shirt from the duffel. "Where do you think you're going?"

"Anywhere Tito is *not*." He snatched the shirt from her and stuffed it back into the bag, then marched across the hall to the bathroom.

Arms folded, Mom blocked the doorway, watching tight-lipped as he scraped his grooming supplies into a shaving kit. "Are you going to tell me what's going on?"

"Dad can explain." He started to push past her, then forced himself to pause and take a breath. "I'm sorry, Mom. Don't worry about me, okay? I have some things to figure out, and I can't do it here."

He knew she'd worry anyway, but she merely nodded and stepped aside. He gave her a quick kiss on the cheek before heading out to his truck.

Not that he had a clue where to go—maybe a room at the Cadwallader? At the rates they charged, though, he couldn't stay for long. But he couldn't exactly leave Gabriel Bend while he had rescue horses to tend to.

He also couldn't stomach the idea of being that close to Lindsey while knowing how much pain it would cause them. On the way into town, he phoned Dalton, the teen volunteer who'd been out a couple of times to help muck stalls and exercise the rescues. The kid had a good head on his shoulders and knew a thing or two about horses.

"I've, uh, had something come up," he told Dalton. "I'll be able to see to the horses first thing every morning, but could you take over evening chores the next few days till I figure out something else?"

When the boy agreed, Spencer told him about the new mares and said he'd leave written instructions in the feed room. He'd make sure to get out there plenty early each day before Lindsey and Audra were up.

The details of checking into the inn and finding his room were enough to keep his mind temporarily occupied. He tossed his hat and duffel onto the bed, then twirled the rolling desk chair around and plopped down. Taking out his phone again, he called his brother. "Hope I'm not interrupting some big real estate deal."

"Uh, not exactly. The new year's starting out kind of slow, and anyway..." Samuel cleared his throat. "Never mind me. What's up with you?"

"I moved out."

Silence. Then, "What happened?"

He told him, every last painful detail. "I've had it, Slam. I get now why you left."

"Tito's part of it, sure. But I had other reasons."

"I think I know those, too." Spencer let himself slide downward until his head rested on the chair back. "Bottom line—we have a dysfunctional family, and I'm through being a part of it."

Samuel snorted. "So you're going to slink away and let Tito have the last word? Come on, Spiny, this is Lindsey we're talking about. The girl you've been crazy about forever. Don't let a grumpy old man and his stupid feud ruin this for you."

"It's already too late. She's done with me."

"Give her time to cool off. She'll realize what you two mean to each other."

"Won't matter if they lose the ranch and she leaves Gabriel Bend."

Samuel tried to encourage him, but with nothing left to say and nothing his brother could do to fix things, Spencer ended the call. After kicking off his boots, he propped himself up in bed, grabbed the remote and flipped channels until he landed on a mind-numbing documentary about the life cycle of mosquitoes.

Perfect, since he felt about as small as a mosquito and as deserving of being squashed like a bug.

For the next two mornings, Spencer's plan to avoid Lindsey succeeded. Setting his alarm for four o'clock, he made it out to the McClement ranch early enough to give his rescues their morning feeding, then take them out to pasture and be on his way before any sign of activity at the house.

That all changed on Saturday, when he flipped the switch for the barn light and found Audra sitting on a tack trunk with her knees drawn up beneath a fuzzy blanket.

"Morning, Spencer." Her greeting came out on a puff of frosty air. Casting him a sad smile, she straightened and lowered her feet to the floor. "Think you could avoid us forever?"

He shrugged. "Thought it would be easier for everyone."

"Then you thought wrong."

One of the horses whinnied. He sidled past Audra toward the feed room. "Just so you know, I'm looking for another place to stable my rescues. Soon as I find one—"

"I'm not worried about that." Dropping the blanket onto the trunk, Audra followed him into the narrow room.

He halted with his back to her and breathed in the earthy smells of grain and hay and equine supplements. For a moment, his mind blanked. Did Ash get the controlled starch feed or the fortified pellets? He glanced at the chalkboard, where he'd written directions for Dalton.

Right, controlled starch for Ash, fortified pellets for the mares. His chin dropped. He hadn't spent enough time with the new girls yet to learn the names their previous owner had given them.

"Spencer."

He jumped when Audra touched his arm.

"You're hurting as much as Lindsey. Don't deny it."

He couldn't if he wanted to.

"Your mom came over yesterday. We had a nice long talk."

Reaching around her, he picked up a scoop and measured out Ash's feed. "Then you should understand why things have to be this way."

"I understand you and Lindsey are victims here. But that doesn't mean the past has to repeat itself." Audra consulted the chalkboard, then found another scoop and filled it with the mares' pellets.

Spencer carried Ash's feed out to his stall and poured it into the tray. Audra followed, dividing her scoop between the two mares. When it was clear she intended to hang around until she'd had her say, he halted and faced her in the middle of the barn aisle. "What do you want me to do, Audra? Nothing's going to change my grandfather, and I can't watch him continue tearing two families apart."

She fisted her hips. "I thought better of you, Spencer Navarro. I thought you were more of a fighter than this."

Her words stung. "Me, a fighter? Where'd you ever get that idea?"

"Because you're the brother who stayed. While

Samuel was off making a life for himself elsewhere, you quietly kept doing your job at home while being a friend to me and to Lindsey even at the risk of your grandfather's disapproval."

"You call that *fighting*?" He pivoted, arms flailing in a gesture of denial. "I call it flying under the radar while trying my level best to keep the peace."

"And now you think turning tail and running is the only option left?" Audra narrowed one eye, appraising him so long that he struggled not to cower. "I was married to a military man, remember? Charles didn't like fighting any more than you do, but the army taught him that to establish lasting peace, sometimes you have to go on the offensive."

He must really be dense, because he had no idea where she was going with this.

"What I'm saying is that I have no intention of rolling over and playing dead so your grandfather can take away my ranch. I haven't told Lindsey yet, but I've decided to fight this injunction with everything I have." Her eyes flashed with determination. "We *will* open our event venue, and it *will* be a roaring success."

She tossed the feed scoop at his chest, then spun on her boot heel and marched out of the barn.

Fumbling both scoops, he stood there momentarily stunned, while her words echoed through his brain. *I thought you were more of a fighter than this.*

Had he been wrong all this time, keeping his head down and living with the status quo instead of doing something to make a difference? Maybe his equine rescue operation was only more of the same—a way of convincing himself he'd chosen his own path, while nothing had actually changed. No matter how he tried to spin it, he still lived under his grandfather's thumb.

It hit him suddenly, what his dad had been trying to say the other day. If Spencer felt constrained by his grandfather's patriarchal iron hand, the pressure on his father must be so much worse.

There had to be a way to break the destructive cycle, and the only way Spencer could think of doing so was to go straight to the source—his grandfather.

Lindsey wished she shared her aunt's confidence that they could beat Arturo Navarro at his intimidation game. If he was that determined to buy the McClement ranch out from under them, maybe they should quit fighting and give him what he wanted. The amount he'd offered through his phony corporation would at least give them a cushion for starting over, and without the stigma of a tax sale or declaring bankruptcy.

In the office Saturday morning, while poring over their dismal financial situation yet again, she said as much to Audra.

Her aunt, usually so quick to remind Lindsey to have faith, scoffed and shook her head. "You two make quite the pair."

Lindsey stifled a groan. Who else could Audra mean except her and Spencer? Yesterday she'd come home from buying groceries to find Lois Navarro leaving. Afterward, Audra told her what Lois had said about Spencer being so upset that he'd packed a few things and taken a room at the Cadwallader. He only tended his rescue horses when he could be certain of not running into Lindsey and was already looking for another boarding facility.

She tossed aside her pencil. "I'm only trying to look at this pragmatically, which I haven't done since I got here. I'm only sorry I dragged you into my fantasy of riding in on my white horse and saving the ranch."

"You didn't drag me. I was more than willing to believe we could do it." Audra fixed Lindsey with a hard stare. "Still am, in fact. *I'm* sorry my new partner is ready to give up so easily."

The truth stabbed deep. With this attitude, Lindsey was no better than her cowardly, traitorous father. Or had Dad actually spoken wisely when he'd talked about being realistic? What was that old saying about beating a dead horse?

Striding to the window, Audra looked toward the Navarro ranch. "I'd hoped I could get through…" Her voice trailed off, and she glanced back at Lindsey with the flicker of a smile. "Or maybe I did after all."

"What are you muttering about?" Lindsey joined her at the window. Nothing looked any different across the way. Except, wasn't that Spencer's truck parked beside the house? "Something else you're not telling me?"

Audra touched a finger to her chin. "You know, those bananas we bought the other day are about ripe enough for banana bread. Think I'll go whip up a batch."

To her aunt's retreating back, she snapped, "Baking is not going to excuse you from answering my question."

She was ready to chase down Audra and insist on an explanation when her cell phone rang. Joella's name appeared on the display. She answered more gruffly than she'd intended.

Her friend choked out a surprised laugh. "Uh, should I call back later?"

"No, I'm sorry. It's been a frustrating few days." Lindsey returned to the desk chair and swiveled toward the window. What had Audra meant? *Was* something going on with the Navarros?

"Want to talk about it?"

"Not really." For one thing, she couldn't scrape up the energy to rehash everything. "Suffice it to say things around here are not going according to plan."

"Oh." The word came out in two disappointed-sounding syllables. "I hope you don't mean the event venue. Not that I'd rather you told me things aren't working out with Spencer, because I always believed you two would get together someday—"

"How about all of the above?"

There was silence on Joella's end. Then, "Now you *have* to tell me what's going on."

Cornered, she gave a quick rundown about Arturo's attempts to buy the ranch and how he'd halted the photo shoot. "Oh, and did I mention my dad signed over his share of the ranch to me? Now, whatever happens, I'm fully committed. Audra wants us to keep fighting, but I'm no longer convinced it's worth it."

Joella gasped. "*Not worth it?* Who *is* this, and what have you done with my friend, the dauntless Lindsey McClement?"

"This Lindsey McClement is tired and doesn't want to talk about it anymore." She stretched out her legs and crossed her ankles. "Cheer me up. Tell me what's going on in your life."

"Not sure I should, under the circumstances."

"Jo-Jo?" Lindsey furrowed her brow.

"I did it, Linds. I quit my job. I've already started packing my apartment, and I was hoping…"

Pulling herself erect, Lindsey clutched her stomach. "Oh, Jo-Jo, you'd actually decided to move here and work with me? I didn't realize—"

"It's my fault. I should have talked to you first before burning my bridges. My last client nearly did me in, and on top of everything else—" Joella released a sharp sigh. "Anyway, the idea of starting over with you in a quiet little place like Gabriel Bend sounded better and better all the time."

"There's nothing I'd like more. But the way things are going, the chances of River Bend Events opening at all are pretty much nonexistent." Lindsey's next words almost choked her. "By March first, there may not even be a McClement ranch anymore."

"Now I *know* you've done something with the real Lindsey McClement. Get one of those extra guest rooms ready—no, better make it two. Because I'm hanging up right now and phoning Holly. Looks like it'll take both of us to keep you from waving the white flag of surrender."

"Joella—" The "call ended" tone sounded in Lindsey's ear. Heart thumping, she lowered the phone and stared at the screen. Would her two best friends really come all the way to Gabriel Bend to make sure she didn't give up on this dream?

She thought back to their days in high school and how when one of them was down, the other two would lovingly push and prod until discouragement vanished and confidence returned.

Groaning, she heaved herself out of the chair. "Audra? Can you handle a few more houseguests?"

Chapter Fourteen

Admitting he needed to confront his grandfather was one thing. Digging up the courage to do so? Something else entirely. It had still been dark Saturday morning when Spencer finished with his rescue horses. Afterward, he'd driven the country roads for more than an hour while sorting through his thoughts and rehearsing what he wanted to say. How did he tell someone he'd looked up to all his life that the man's recent actions made Spencer ashamed to call him family?

By the time the sun had fully risen, he was as ready as he'd ever be. Even so, he made himself wait another couple of hours before heading to the Navarro ranch. It wouldn't help his case to show up while Dad and the stable hands grappled with covering morning chores in the wake of Spencer's abrupt departure.

But now that he was here, the weight of his decision sat on his shoulders like a crushing boulder. Mom, of course, had been glad to have him home. Though he told her he wouldn't be staying any longer than it took to say his piece to Tito, she immediately plied him with buttery scrambled eggs and a mug of his favorite cinnamon-laced coffee.

"You have to eat," she insisted, adding four link sausages to his plate. "I can only imagine the junk food you've been subsisting on in town."

She wasn't wrong. But this morning he had no appetite, his stomach curdling with anxiety about the confrontation awaiting him.

As he forced down a forkful of eggs, Dad stormed in. "So you're back. About time you called an end to this temper tantrum and returned to your responsibilities."

"That isn't why I came." Spencer clenched a fist. "I thought after our talk—"

"Which you walked out on."

"Yes, and I'm sorry about that." Pushing away from the table, Spencer stood and braced his knuckles on either side of his plate. "My feelings haven't changed, but I've realized I won't be able to move forward, whatever I decide to do with my life, until I clear the air with Tito."

Behind him, his grandfather gave a loud *harrumph*. "Then say what you have come to say."

Spencer spun around, suddenly unsure whether he could get the words out. Few people could make him feel as inept and inadequate as his grandfather could. "Tito, I—"

"You have come home to apologize, I assume." Tito crossed the kitchen and poured himself a mug of coffee. Turning, he graced Spencer with a condescending smile. "Your infatuation with the McClement girl will pass. You only need to accept your role as a Navarro and—"

"No."

Tito's brows shot up.

"Son…" Spencer's father cast him a warning frown, but his eyes clouded with a different emotion. Fear?

Giving her head a small shake, Mom sidled over to Dad and linked her arm through his. After a sharp exhalation, he clamped his lips together as if accepting the inevitable.

Spencer let out a tremulous breath in a struggle to keep his voice level. "I love you, Tito. All my life, I've wanted nothing more than to make you and Dad proud. Excellence in horsemanship, integrity in business dealings— it's a legacy I've tried my best to honor."

Pausing, he drew a hand across his face. *God, give me strength. Give me the words.*

He stood a little taller, his gaze locked with his grandfather's. "It took me a long time to understand how Samuel could leave like he did, and just like you and Dad, I resented him for turning his back on the family business. But he was only trying to protect himself, and now I've got to do the same. I can no longer be part of a family who would choose bitterness and greed over compromise and forgiveness."

Tito froze, a stricken look replacing the smug smile he'd worn moments ago. The hand holding the coffee mug shook slightly. "You—you would not say such things if you knew—"

"Don't try to justify what you've done to people I care about. To people *you* should have loved enough to treat with compassion and respect." Spencer sliced the air with his hand. "And all because of something so far in the past that nobody remembers what started it."

In the split second before Tito's coffee mug would have hit the floor, Spencer's dad rushed forward and grabbed it, the hot liquid splashing onto his hand. Wincing, he shot Spencer a distracted frown. "That's enough. You should go."

With everything else he'd meant to say logjamming in his throat, Spencer took a hard look at his grandfather, only then noticing the man's pallor. Perspiration dotted Tito's brow. He'd mashed his lips so tightly together that they'd turned white.

As Dad helped Tito to a chair, Mom reached for the kitchen phone. Hanging up after a frantic call, she said, "An ambulance will take too long. His doctor said to give him an aspirin and drive him straight to the ER in Georgetown."

"You will do no such thing," Tito argued as one hand clutched his chest.

All other thoughts evaporating, Spencer strode to the door. "I can take him in my truck. It's right outside."

Mom coaxed Tito to chew and swallow the aspirin. "Help your dad walk him out. I'll grab a pillow and blanket."

Minutes later, they'd made Tito as comfortable as possible in the passenger seat. With Georgetown's St. David's Hospital at least half an hour away, Spencer wasted no time hitting the road. His parents followed in Mom's car.

The medical team quickly confirmed a heart attack, and Spencer collapsed in a waiting room chair. This was his fault. He'd known Tito hadn't been well, yet he'd unloaded on him anyway. *God, why didn't You stop me?*

Like anyone could have, in his current state of mind. But did Tito's heart attack change anything? Mom had even mentioned the other day her surprise that something like this hadn't happened sooner. No, as guilt-ridden as Spencer felt for his part in bringing this on, he wouldn't accept blame for the spiritual condition of his grandfather's heart. That, Arturo Navarro had allowed on his own.

It was well past one o'clock before a doctor came to tell them Tito's condition had stabilized but that further tests and treatment would be necessary, possibly even bypass surgery. "We're admitting him to the coronary care unit right now. Expect him to be in the hospital for several days."

Spencer's dad slid both hands down his face. "But he'll recover?"

"We're doing everything we can to ensure a positive outcome." Doctor-speak for *He's in bad shape, so no promises*.

With a silent prayer of thanks that his grandfather had survived thus far and was in good hands, Spencer backed away, preparing to leave. There was nothing more he could do here.

His father turned. "Where are you going?"

"I still need to find another place to live and somewhere to move my rescues."

Eyes narrowed to mere slits, his father ground his teeth. "In that case, consider your employment with Navarro Quarter Horses officially terminated. Your last paycheck is waiting for you in the barn office. I would prefer that you pick it up while I am not there."

Mom clutched Dad's arm. "Hank, don't—"

"No," he replied, one hand raised, "if our son is determined to go his own way, then that's what he must do." With a dismissive shake of his head, he turned away.

Staring at his father's back, Spencer swallowed the nausea rising in his throat. He'd prayed for at least a scrap of understanding, from his own father if not from

Tito. He'd expected bruised feelings, even anger over his decision. But his grandfather nearly dying, his father essentially disowning him—that hadn't been part of the plan. He'd never felt so utterly forsaken.

As he trudged out to his truck, it dawned on him—with Lindsey's parents divorced and her father out of her life, she could understand better than anyone else how badly he was hurting. He needed her, now more than ever.

Was it too late to fix things between them?

Lindsey had been in the kitchen with Audra when she glanced up to see Spencer and his dad helping Arturo to the truck. Spencer had mentioned his grandfather hadn't been in the best of health lately. The old man had looked feeble and pale. Considering how quickly they'd all driven off, had Arturo's condition taken a dramatic turn for the worse?

She'd been tempted to call and ask if there was anything she could do but wasn't sure Spencer would welcome her intrusion. Audra had no such reservations and had immediately tried to reach Lois. When no one answered, she left a message expressing her concern and offering any assistance the family might need.

The hours since had dragged by. Lindsey tried to stay busy, but there didn't seem much point in agonizing over bills they couldn't pay or making more plans for an event venue that likely would never open. And was Joella serious about her and Holly coming to the ranch, if only for a visit? Joella maybe, but Holly couldn't exactly cancel any pending catering jobs to pop over to Gabriel Bend to cheer up a friend.

Shortly after three o'clock, Lindsey's phone buzzed

in her pocket. Hoping against hope it might be Spencer, she nearly dropped the phone before she could read the display.

Not Spencer. Holly. Lindsey answered with a weak hello.

"Wow, don't sound so excited to hear from me."

"Sorry, I thought it might be—" Her voice cracked.

"Spencer?" Holly sighed. "Joella told me things aren't going great for you right now."

"It gets worse." Lindsey confided her worries about Spencer's grandfather. "Much as I despise the way he's treated us, I certainly don't wish him ill."

"Of course not. I'll add my prayers to yours." After a slight pause, Holly continued, "I'm also praying this folderol with the court order blows over...because ever since we talked last, I've also been talking to Joella and thinking a lot."

From the living room window, Lindsey peered out at the gloomy afternoon. An icy rain had begun to fall. Just what they needed—slick roads and the possibility of a power failure. "I know I was trying to talk you both into coming and working with me here, but now..."

"Joella told me how close you are to giving up. But don't. Please." Holly's voice took on a desperate tone. "Things aren't going so well for me right now either. A new catering franchise opened up in town last fall, and they're slowly eating up—pardon the pun—the home-grown businesses like mine."

"Oh, Holly..."

"But I believe in you, Lindsey. Even more, I believe in what the three of us—you, me, Joella—could accomplish together. You said it yourself. By combining our talents, we have everything we need to develop a successful event venue."

Lindsey's throat tightened. "Not if the court order sticks."

Holly grew quiet for a moment. "I hate to even say this, but if Mr. Navarro's so sick…"

"Don't go there. This is Spencer's grandfather we're talking about." She'd barely spoken the words when she glimpsed Spencer's truck passing by. Her heart twisted as she watched him turn into his family's driveway.

"I get it," Holly said, apology in her tone. "I can only imagine how preoccupied you must be. I shouldn't have added more pressure."

"It's okay. And I'll always be grateful for your vote of confidence. If anything does change, you'll be the first to know. But…don't count on it."

Holly expressed her understanding and promised to keep praying for everyone's best.

As Lindsey ended the call, Audra came in from the kitchen. Tugging on her parka and gloves, she said, "The rain's turning to sleet. I'm going to move the cows to the near pasture for the night and put out more hay."

"I can help." Lindsey followed her aunt back through the house and grabbed her jacket and gloves.

Starting for the barn, Audra motioned Lindsey toward the equipment shed. "We can get this done a lot faster if I saddle up and bring in the cows while you load a couple of hay bales into the Mule and drive it over."

"Will do. Be careful out there!"

At Audra's brisk nod, Lindsey jogged over and started up the Mule. With sleet peppering the roof, she backed up to the shed where they stored hay and shavings, then climbed out and shoved open the heavy sliding door.

Her heart plummeted. When had they used up the last of their hay?

Clambering into the driver's seat again, she steered the vehicle across the yard and halted in front of the main barn. She jumped out and raced inside, where her aunt finished knotting the cinch on Skeeter's saddle. "We have a problem. The hay shed's empty."

Audra looked up, panic etching her face. "Oh, no. I saw we were running low last week, but I didn't realize—" She pressed a fist to her lips. "I've run up such a huge bill with our supplier that I kept putting off calling him again."

Lindsey had seen the past-due invoices. Another had arrived in yesterday's mail, and only this morning she'd remitted a small check in hopes the supplier wouldn't cut off their account completely. One hand on her hip, the other at her forehead, she racked her brain. Outside, the sleet came down even harder. The animals needed hay, but only a partial bale remained in the feed room. Somehow, she had to come up with a way to get more—and quickly.

"Bring in the cattle," she told her aunt. "I'll figure out…something."

Giving her head a doubtful shake, Audra swung up into the saddle, then nudged Skeeter's sides and rode out.

As Lindsey watched her aunt disappear into the wintry precipitation, she could think of only one possibility—they'd have to borrow from the Navarros. Despite everything, surely Spencer wouldn't turn them down.

Hunched over in the chair, forehead resting on the barn office desk, Spencer held his sides against unbearable heartache. He'd sat there for the better part of an hour, debating whether to take the money he'd rightfully earned, or leave it in the drawer as testament to his ultimate break with his family. Leaving them at the hospital had been the most painful goodbye of his life.

The vibration of his cell phone propelled him upright. With a sigh, he checked the display—Samuel. He pressed the answer button. "Guess you heard."

"Mom called a little bit ago," his twin said. "But frankly, she sounded more worried about you than she did about Tito. Still staying at the inn? I can be there in a few hours."

"No, don't. The weather's turning bad here. You shouldn't be on the roads." Spencer massaged his aching eyes. "Nothing you could do anyway."

"I don't like the way you sound, Spiny. You shouldn't be facing this by yourself."

Spencer couldn't hold back a sardonic laugh.

"I'm serious," Samuel stated, his voice rising. "Call Lindsey. Work things out."

"Not happening. I told you, it's too late."

The words had barely left his lips when a motion outside caught his eye. It couldn't be—*Lindsey?*

Whatever Samuel said in response, Spencer didn't hear. "I have to go." He clicked off and tossed his phone onto the desk.

Lindsey must have noticed the light on in the office. She'd parked the Mule outside the barn, then rushed inside, almost crashing into him as he exited the office. It would have felt so natural to reach up and brush the ice particles from her tangled curls. Instead, he fisted his hands at his sides.

"Spencer, I, um…" She backed up, her teeth chattering. "We're out of hay. I wouldn't ask, but the cows need it to make it through the freeze, and I was hoping—"

"As much as you need, it's yours." He gestured toward the office. "Go in and get warm. I was going to bring over a couple more bales for my rescues anyway, so I'll load up the back of my truck."

"Wait—you don't have a coat."

He hadn't even noticed. While he stood there feeling like an idiot, Lindsey darted into the room. She came out with the sherpa-lined denim jacket he'd been wearing earlier, along with his black felt Stetson. By the time he'd jammed his arms into the jacket sleeves, the cold had begun to penetrate.

She handed him his hat, then jogged toward his truck. Over her shoulder, she called, "We'll get done faster if we work together."

He should have learned long ago not to argue with Lindsey McClement.

With Lindsey in the passenger seat, he drove the truck down the lane to the open-sided hay barn. Working in tandem, they loaded ten bales into the bed. Lindsey promised to either replace the bales they used once they could order more or reimburse him for the cost.

Back in the truck, Lindsey reached across suddenly to clutch Spencer's forearm. "I feel awful for not asking right away—did something happen with your grandfather this morning? Is he all right?"

"It's his heart. He may need a bypass." As Spencer pulled onto the road, the truck skidded on the icy pavement. He eased off the accelerator until the tires found traction as Lindsey white-knuckled the armrest.

She relaxed slightly when they turned up her gravel

driveway. "A bypass sounds serious. I'm so sorry, Spencer."

"Thanks." Not much more he could say.

Up ahead, he caught sight of Audra riding Skeeter as she herded the last cow through the far gate. He backed up to the barn-side gate so they could open it to the inside and unload hay bales without the cattle getting out.

Audra rode over, cheeks red from the cold and sleet speckling her stocking cap and parka. "Oh, Spencer, are you a sight for sore eyes!"

"Glad to help." Climbing into the truck bed, he hefted a bale and heaved it into the pasture.

Lindsey and Audra went to work separating and distributing the hay while Spencer started on another one. Once the cows were taken care of, Spencer moved his truck over to Audra's hay shed and stacked the remaining bales inside. As he finished, his cell phone rang.

It was Dalton, his volunteer. "My mom won't let me drive in this weather. I'm real sorry, but I can't make it this afternoon."

"Don't worry about it. I had to come out for something else anyway." No need to explain further. "I'll let you know if I need you tomorrow."

He'd barely disconnected when his phone rang again. This time it was his mother. "My friend-finder app says you're at home." He'd forgotten she could follow him that way. "Honey, I know you're still angry and upset, and your dad didn't want me to call, but with the roads icing up, we need to stay in Georgetown tonight, close to the hospital. Just for now, would you handle things there?"

Ducking out of the wind, he tugged his jacket collar higher around his neck. "Sure, Mom. Tell Dad I've got it under control."

"I knew we could count on you. I love you, son."

He swallowed. "How's Tito?"

She waited too long to answer. "I've never seen your dad so worried."

As they said their goodbyes, he looked up to see Lindsey hurrying over. She frowned as he tucked away his phone. "Is everything okay?"

"My parents are at the hospital. Dad left me in charge until he can get back." He moved around her. "I need to feed my rescues, and then I'll get out of your way."

"Let me take care of them for you." She jogged up beside him. "After you came to our rescue this afternoon, it's the least I can do."

He halted so suddenly that she skidded past and almost tripped. When he steadied her, warmth shot up his arm, even through her coat sleeve and his leather glove. Throat clenching, he dropped his hand but held her gaze. "You don't owe me anything. Ever."

For a long moment, she silently stared at him, a complicated mixture of pain and confusion and concern in her huge brown eyes. She brushed away the ice crystals clinging to her brows and lashes. "Then as your friend, let me help."

"Okay. Thanks." With a brisk nod, he strode back to his truck.

Chapter Fifteen

Lindsey awoke Sunday morning to a winter wonderland. Icicles hung from the eaves, and every tree branch glistened like crystal in the slanting sunlight of dawn. The roads would be too treacherous for driving into town for church. At least they still had power.

From outside her window came the crunch of boots on icy ground. Bundled into her flannel robe and fuzzy slippers, she peeked through the blinds and saw Spencer heading into the barn. Naturally, he'd want to see to his rescue horses first thing.

Turning away, she gave her head a sad shake. The man was loyal to a fault. Despite the animosity ripping his family apart, he'd stepped up when his father needed him and had returned home to manage the ranch. How could she not admire such selflessness?

How could she not admit she'd fallen hopelessly in love with Spencer Navarro?

"Dear God…" Eyes lifted heavenward, she sank onto the bed. "I want to trust You, but with all the things that have gone wrong in my life, it hasn't been easy. Please, can't You show me a way out of this mess?" *Please, show me a way Spencer and I can be together!*

With no flashing neon lights revealing God's answer, Lindsey heaved a resigned sigh. After dressing in jeans and a thick sweatshirt, she headed downstairs. A pot of coffee was already brewed, which meant Audra had gotten her usual early start. Lindsey wasn't sure she'd ever get used to prying herself out of bed before dawn to begin ranch chores, especially in the cold.

On the other hand, if things didn't change in their favor soon, she needn't be concerned with feeding livestock or mucking stalls in any kind of weather.

Her stomach clenched at the thought. She set down the mug she'd filled and hunched over the counter.

The back door swung open, letting in a wintry draft. Audra bustled in and quickly shut the door. "It's freezing out there!"

Straightening with a forced smile, Lindsey poured another mug of coffee and handed it to her aunt. "When will I ever convince you to wake me up so I can help?"

"You know I'm on automatic pilot first thing in the morning, just doing what needs doing." Audra took several sips of coffee before setting down the mug to peel off her coat and gloves. "Spencer could use some help today, though. He told me several of the Navarro ranch hands aren't going to make it in to work."

Lindsey wasn't sure how much use she'd be, but she did owe him for the hay after all.

Or…could the ice storm have been God's "flashing neon" answer to at least one of her prayers? It had certainly given her a reason to reach past the barriers between her and Spencer so they could try to be friends again. Whatever else happened, she couldn't bear the thought of living at odds with him.

After a quick breakfast of toast and juice, she poured her coffee into a travel mug and hiked across the field to the gap in the barbed-wire fence. Climbing through, she glimpsed Spencer trundling a manure cart out of the main barn.

When she caught up with him at the collection bin, he looked around in surprise. "Need something?"

She shrugged. "Heard you were shorthanded today. What can I do?"

He glanced away for a moment as if intending to refuse her offer. Then he looked back at her with skewed lips. "What I could really use help with is the stack of inventory lists my dad left in the barn office. Everything has to be entered in a spreadsheet, and…" He grimaced. "You know me and computers."

"I can do that. You'll have to tell me how to log on and access the file."

"Should be a paper with instructions in the center desk drawer." He patted his coat pocket. "I have my cell if you run into problems."

Sitting behind a desk in a warm office while Spencer handled the outdoor chores in twenty-five-degree weather didn't exactly sound fair, but then, he knew horses and she knew spreadsheets. Plus, working separately would lessen the awkwardness.

She found the inventory lists under a paperweight and could easily understand why this much data entry would intimidate Spencer. Opening the drawer, she poked around in search of the instructions he'd mentioned. Lots of pens and pencils, rubber bands, paper clips, crumpled cash register receipts, a thin stack of payroll envelopes banded together, but no computer instructions.

Without being too nosy, she checked the other drawers without success. Before phoning Spencer, she decided to try the center drawer one more time. Maybe the instruction page was jammed in the back. When she pulled the drawer completely out, an accordioned sheet of lined paper fell to the floor. As she bent to retrieve it, something else caught her eye—an old photograph stuck beneath the drawer runner. She worked the snapshot free, then gasped in astonishment at the two grinning faces looking back at her.

"Grandpa?" It had to be. And the man with one arm draped around Grandpa's shoulder could only be Arturo Navarro. The men, looking to be in their midtwenties, stood proudly between the two pillars of a crudely built ranch gate made of stone and cedar. Emblazoned on the arched crosspiece above them were the words *Rancho de Manos y Corazón.*

Tears sprang to Lindsey's eyes. There was no misreading the closeness between these men—their mutual affection cemented with ambition, courage and determination. She stared for a long time at the photo, wondering how two such devoted friends could have turned into bitter enemies.

She was still pondering the past when Spencer walked in. "How's it go—" He broke off as their eyes met. "What's wrong?"

"Look." She handed him the photo and watched his expression cycle through the same emotions she'd felt.

He ran his gloved thumb across his chin. "Where'd you find this?"

She pointed to the drawer. "It was stuck underneath. I didn't mean to snoop, but I couldn't find…"

"It's fine." Spencer sank into a chair across from her, his gaze never leaving the photo. After a long stretch of silence, he murmured, "Those inventory records can wait. Why don't you go on home. I, uh, have some thinking to do."

Quietly, Lindsey rose and reached for her coat. At the door, she turned, an ache in her throat. "Will you be all right?"

Without looking up, he nodded and waved a hand.

She slipped out, closing the door behind her. The cold air shocked her lungs, but the sun had melted some of the icy patches. The Mule still sat where she'd parked it yesterday when she'd come over to ask for hay, so she climbed in to drive it home. Maneuvering cautiously along the road, she slowed to turn up her driveway, then braked as her attention landed on the two crumbling piles of stone on either side of the entrance. How many times had she passed them by without a second thought?

But today she recognized them for what they were— the bases for the cedar posts that once supported the original ranch gate, shown in the photo she'd found. *Rancho de Manos y Corazón*—Hands and Heart Ranch.

Was *this* the neon sign she'd prayed God would send her? A message from the past to restore hope for the future?

Around ten o'clock, two of the Navarro ranch hands made it in to work. Sundays were slow days, mainly a matter of cleaning stalls and giving fresh hay, feed and water. With the wind dying down and the sun melting the ice and warming the temperature above freezing, Spencer had no concerns about turning the horses out to pasture. Once he'd seen to the animals requiring specialized attention or exercise, he left instructions with the men for the rest of the afternoon. After handing them their pay envelopes, he headed toward Georgetown.

His grandfather may not want to see him, but with God's help, perhaps this time he could get through to the old man—before it was too late for them both.

A hospital volunteer at the front desk directed him to his grandfather's room. He rapped softly on the half-closed door, then eased it open. He found his father sitting next to the bed, where Tito lay softly snoring.

Dad looked up from the newspaper he'd been reading. "Everything under control at the ranch?"

"Everything's fine." Spencer chewed the inside of his lip. "Where's Mom?"

"Resting at the hotel." Dad went back to reading the paper.

He edged closer, the old photograph practically burning a hole in his shirt pocket. A small monitor near the bed beeped softly as it traced his grandfather's heart rhythm. The squiggly lines didn't mean much to Spencer, but he hoped the apparent regularity of the blips was a positive sign. "Has Tito been awake at all?"

"Some. He's supposed to be—"

Tito stirred. "Is that my grandson?"

"Yes, it's me. Spencer." He took a hesitant step toward the bed.

"Come…closer." With one veined hand, his grandfather weakly patted the mattress.

Dad rose and tossed his newspaper into the chair.

"You should be resting, Papi." To Spencer, he murmured, "This is not the time to get him agitated."

"Let us talk," Tito insisted. "Leave us, Enrique."

With a huff and a tight-lipped glare, Spencer's father strode out to the corridor.

Tito nodded toward the chair Spencer's father had vacated. "Sit."

Second-guessing his intentions, Spencer looked at the monitor, where the blips seemed to be coming faster. "I don't want to tire you, Tito. After you're better, we can—"

"I may not get better. That's why we must talk." Urgency shone in his heavy-lidded eyes. He reached for Spencer's hand, clasping it in his dry and calloused one. "Your father needs you. He cannot manage the ranch alone."

Spencer took a long, slow breath. "I tried to tell you why I can't stay."

"Yes, I know. You are angry that I intervened with the neighbors' plans. But if I withdraw my complaint and allow them to go forward with this—this business venture they have in mind, will you then come home and fulfill your responsibilities?"

Why did his grandfather's offer sound like there were strings attached? With one eye on the monitor, Spencer said, "I know about Aunt Alicia and Owen McClement. I know you kept them apart. I won't let you do the same to me and Lindsey."

"It was for my daughter's best, as it will be for yours." Tito's grip tightened. "The ranch will belong to you one day. Don't turn your back on your inheritance like your brother did."

"It's not about the inheritance, Tito. And it's not that I haven't loved every minute working alongside you and

Dad and learning everything I can from you. But it's not enough anymore. I need the freedom to follow my heart. To be with the woman I love."

Mouth firm, Tito shook his head. "You're young. Idealistic. But given time, you will come to see—"

"What I see," Spencer interrupted, his tone gentle, "is a sick old man who's given his life over to bitterness. I don't think you realize everything it's cost you." Closing his eyes briefly, he pulled the photo from his pocket. He studied it for a few seconds before slipping it into his grandfather's hand. "Idealism isn't a bad thing, Tito. Maybe this will help you remember."

Brows pinched together, Tito held the photo up to the light. His lower lip began to tremble. A tear trickled from the corner of his eye, and he clutched the picture to his heart. "Ah, my old friend. If only…things had been different…"

The door whispered open, and Spencer's father peered into the room. He looked first at Tito, then at the heart monitor, before shooting Spencer a concerned frown. "What did you say to him?"

"Just reminded him who he used to be." He stood. "I'll go now."

"Wait." Dad caught Spencer's elbow. "I haven't often shown you the appreciation you deserve, and I know you're only doing what you feel you must. So I'll ask this one time only. Please. Come home. Let me try to set things right. Between us…" He lowered his voice. "And with Mrs. Forrester and her niece."

With a glance back at his grandfather, still cradling the snapshot as he stared at something unseen, Spencer sighed. "I'm hopeful we've taken a step in that direction." He drew his father into a hug. "Sure, Dad, see you at home later. We'll talk more then."

Grunting in surprise, Dad patted Spencer's back. "Yes, son. Yes, we will. I—I love you."

Spencer wasn't sure he could remember the last time his father had actually spoken those words aloud. "I love you, too, Dad. Hope you know that."

On his way to the exit, he had to brush something wet off his cheek. Crossing the lobby, he glimpsed his mother coming toward him. Lindsey and Audra followed on either side of her.

"Hi, honey," she said. "Look who I ran into in the parking lot."

Audra took his hand, stretching tall to brush a kiss across his cheek. "The roads were clear, so we wanted to drive over and see how y'all are doing."

"That's nice of you." He spoke to Audra, but his gaze was locked with Lindsey's. She'd hung back, uncertainty in her eyes.

As Audra moved aside, Mom linked her arm through his, her brow knit. "I wasn't expecting to see you here today. Did you look in on your grandfather?"

"Yeah." Giving himself a mental shake, he returned his attention to his mother. "He was awake for a bit. Dad's with him now."

"We don't want to intrude," Audra said. "But if we can run any errands for you, bring over some takeout, anything at all—"

Shifting her glance between Spencer and Lindsey, Mom gave a knowing smile. "Audra, how about joining me for coffee in the cafeteria? I think these kids could use some alone time."

Eyes widening, Audra nodded. "Good idea."

As the two women headed down the corridor, Spencer turned to Lindsey with a hesitant smile, then gestured toward a pair of empty chairs in the far corner of the lobby. Without a word, she fell into step beside him.

Once they were seated, he reached for her hand. Staring at her fingertips, he said, "My grandfather told me if I'd come back to the ranch, he'd cancel his complaint and you could proceed with your plans."

She stiffened. "I hated that you left in the first place because of me. I'm sorry I ever doubted you, but I'd never ask you to agree just so we could go ahead with the event venue."

"That's essentially the deal my grandfather had in mind until…" He raised his eyes to meet hers. "I gave him the picture."

She sucked in a breath. "How did he react?"

"I saw a spark of the man who once knew your grandfather as a friend, and it gave me hope this feud will one day be over." He shifted so their knees were touching. "But whatever the future holds, I want you to know I'll always fight for you. For your hopes and dreams and plans and happiness."

"And your own hopes and dreams?" Tenderness filled her expression. "What makes you happy, Spencer?"

He lifted a hand to gently tuck a curl behind her ear. "You."

Hands clammy, heart hammering, Lindsey had to remind herself to breathe. Was her dearest dream closer than ever to coming true? "Wh-what are you saying, Spencer?"

Glancing around the lobby, he uttered a nervous laugh. "You're going to make me spell it out? Right here in public?"

"Uh, yeah, I think I am. Because with witnesses, you'll have a much harder time taking it back." She winked.

"Okay, then." He cleared his throat and dropped to one knee in front of her.

When every eye in the lobby turned their way, she felt her face turn twenty shades of red. "Spencer," she rasped, "what are you doing?"

"Spelling it out. In public, like you asked. Because you deserve at least that much." He hadn't let go of her hand. Speaking loudly enough to be heard across the room, he said, "Lindsey McClement, I'm crazy in love with you. Always have been. I didn't think this through soon enough to have a ring for your finger, but I'm asking anyway. Will you step into the uncertain future with me and say you'll be my wife?"

Uncertain didn't begin to describe her feelings. She couldn't be more certain about her love for this man, but did she dare hope they could overcome all the obstacles still standing in their way? Tears forming, she slowly shook her head. "I don't know… I'm so scared."

She sensed more than heard the collective *awwww* from the onlookers hanging on their every word.

"I'm scared, too," Spencer said. He pushed up from the floor, then pulled her to her feet. With one arm at her waist, he took her hand and laid it upon his chest. "But my heart's beating with enough courage for both of us. All you have to do is say yes."

She looked into his eyes, and everyone else in the room disappeared as she murmured a contented "Yes."

Spencer lowered his smiling lips to hers in the kiss it seemed she'd been waiting for half her life. With one hand still centered on his heart, the other creeping up to cradle his head, she returned his kiss with all the love she'd been holding inside all these years.

And then they were no longer lost in their own private world, because everyone in the lobby was applauding and cheering. The heat of her blush returning, Lindsey dipped her chin and snuggled deeper into Spencer's protective embrace.

When she looked up again, she glimpsed Audra and Lois among their delighted audience. Both women were beaming as they hurried over.

"About time," Audra said, pulling Lindsey into a hug.

"I'll say." Lois hooked an arm around Spencer's neck and planted a kiss on his cheek.

"Um, this is getting embarrassing." Lindsey tugged at a strand of hair. "Maybe we could go somewhere a little more private?"

"Now the woman wants privacy," Spencer quipped, but she could tell from the edge to his tone that he'd had about all the attention he could handle, too. "Actually, I should be getting back to the ranch before the stable hands knock off for the day." He drew Lindsey closer, his voice dropping to an intimate whisper. "Save some time for me this evening?"

"Count on it."

Lindsey knew better than to expect their problems to suddenly be resolved because they'd admitted their feelings and committed to making a life together. Even so, she couldn't help being hopeful. Arriving home later that afternoon, she kept an eye out for Spencer, knowing he'd be over eventually to take care of his rescue horses. She couldn't wait to be in his arms once more, to be convinced all over again that he really had asked her to marry him.

And she'd really said yes!

The evening sun was just settling behind the hills when she glimpsed him loping across the field. Grabbing her jacket, she scurried out the back door and met him at the barn. He threw his arms around her and kissed her until they were both breathless.

"I have good news," he said when he finally let her go. "Mom called a few minutes ago on their way home from the hospital. Tito won't need a bypass after all. He was doing a lot better this afternoon."

"That's…good." She wanted to be happy for Spencer's grandfather, but if his health improved, would his bitterness return as well?

"And that's not all." With his hands locked around Lindsey's waist, he grinned down at her. "Tito had Dad call his attorney—who apparently wasn't real happy about having his Sunday afternoon interrupted—and told him to drop the nuisance complaint."

"What?" A bubble of excitement swelled Lindsey's throat. "You mean—"

"The sheriff's already been notified. It's over. You can open your event venue as soon as you're ready."

"Oh, Spencer, thank you!" She pulled him close for a series of quick kisses. Then, drawing away abruptly, she raised both hands to her cheeks. "Don't go anywhere. I've got to make a phone call, *right now.*"

With Spencer's laughter fading behind her, she ran to the house. In the office, she riffled through the desk for the photography agreement Jenny and Zach had signed. At least she hadn't completely gone berserk and ripped it to shreds the day the deputy had stopped the photo shoot.

Seconds later, she had Jenny on the line. After a brief explanation and assuring her that River Bend Events and Wedding Chapel was back in business, she asked whether the couple had already done their engagement photos.

"No, we haven't," Jenny said. "We were so disappointed after what happened that we hadn't gotten around to rescheduling somewhere else. We'd absolutely love to come back and do them at your place."

"That's wonderful. Check the weather forecast and pick a day that works for you, and we'll be here to help any way we can."

"Thanks so much! And we definitely want to book the chapel for our June wedding. It's exactly what we were looking for."

"I'll save the date for you. We should be full-service by then, with a professional event planner and caterer on-site." Lindsey's next two calls would be to Joella and Holly. If her friends were still planning to visit next weekend, they could sit down for a detailed planning session.

As she ended the call, Audra peeked in. Bouncing on her toes, she told her aunt what had happened.

"What have I been telling you, sweetie?" Audra wrapped her in a hug. "God's got this. Always has, always will."

Catching her breath, Lindsey leaned against the edge of the desk. "Do you suppose Arturo's change of heart means the feud is finally over?"

Audra looked out across the field toward the Navarro ranch. "I'd like to hope so, but I suspect God's got quite a bit more work to do in that department. All we can do is keep praying for him." She turned to Lindsey with a pensive smile. "For all of us."

"I will." She slipped an arm around her aunt's shoulder. "You're an inspiration, you know. When I first got here, my faith was pretty shaky. But you and Spencer have helped me remember that, no matter how bad the situation looks or how long we have to wait for answers, God can be trusted to work things out for the best."

"Exactly. And speaking of Spencer…" Audra nodded toward the window. "He's looking a bit impatient for you to come out."

Lindsey's pulse sped up. She glanced at her phone, then back at Spencer. If she didn't call her friends right away, they'd understand. Because one minute more apart from the man she loved was one minute too long.

Epilogue

Spending Valentine's Day on the road towing a cattle trailer wasn't exactly how Lindsey had envisioned celebrating. She'd much rather be with Spencer sharing some Valentine's kisses and making plans for their future together. They'd decided to get married sooner rather than later and already had the license. With so many other demands on their time, not to mention the remnants of tension between their two families, Spencer had arranged a private ceremony for the following Saturday in his pastor's office. Three days on Galveston Island would have to do for a honeymoon until they could plan a longer vacation.

This Fort Worth cattle-buying trip with Audra had been a celebration in itself. In the few short weeks since the official launch of River Bend Events and Wedding Chapel, word had spread rapidly—thanks in no small part to recommendations from Jenny and Zach as well as their photographer, who'd fallen in love with the ranch and had already brought out five more couples for engagement and bridal photos. With the fees from those sessions, plus deposits to reserve the wedding chapel in the coming months, Lindsey had paid off the ranch's back taxes and had enough left over to buy a few bred heifers to start rebuilding the herd.

Equally exciting, Joella and Holly were in the process of relocating to Gabriel Bend. Holly had found an apartment in town close to the elementary school Davey would attend, and last weekend Joella had moved into a guest room at the ranch. Lindsey held secret hopes that someday Joella and Samuel would get together, but since Samuel spent so little time at the Navarro ranch, playing matchmaker for the couple wouldn't be so easy. On the other hand, God had done just fine working things out for Lindsey and Spencer. If Samuel was the right guy for Joella, God could certainly do the same for them.

The truck jounced over a pothole, jarring Lindsey out of her daydreams. Blinking, she saw they were on the ranch-to-market road only a few miles from home.

"Better wake up," Audra said from behind the wheel. "Might want to fix your hair before you go racing off to see your sweetie first thing."

Lindsey flipped down the visor mirror to check her reflection, only to grimace at her messy ponytail. She ripped off her scrunchie and finger-combed the tangles as best she could. "He'll understand. Hauling cows isn't exactly glamorous work."

Audra smirked and wiggled her brows.

They turned into the McClement driveway as dusk began to fall.

Lindsey sat straighter, surprised to see several vehicles lining the shoulder. "What in the world... Did Joella schedule a last-minute event?"

"Something's going on." Audra didn't seem all that

curious as she maneuvered the truck and trailer into a narrow lane branching off toward one of the pastures. "Get the gate for me, will you? I'll pull all the way in, and then we can get these ladies settled in their new digs."

Lindsey had barely closed the gate behind the trailer when Spencer's equine rescue volunteer jogged over. "Let me help," Dalton said. "You prob'ly want to go freshen up."

"No hurry. But do you know why all these cars are here?"

"Uh…" There was something fishy about Dalton's stiff grin. "I think an event or something?"

She'd guessed that much. "If you don't mind helping with the cows, I should probably see if I'm needed over there."

Audra came around to the rear of the trailer. "Oh, hi, Dalton." Her weird smile matched his. "We're good here, Lindsey. Go on to the house."

"Fine." Heaving an exaggerated shrug, she let herself out the gate. Last-minute event or not, all she really wanted to do was find Spencer.

When Holly and Davey intercepted her on the driveway, she felt sure something strange was going on. "You look exhausted, Linds." Holly linked arms with her and steered her up the front porch steps. "Bet you can't wait to splash some water on your face and change into something a little more…um…"

Davey darted past them and rushed inside. As Lindsey stepped into the entryway, he came toward her with an armful of long-stemmed red roses, which he presented with a gallant bow. "These aren't from me, though," he said with a grin.

"Really?" Lindsey dropped her jaw in feigned surprise. "Then who?" Spencer must have put him up to this.

"Want me to take care of those for you?" Holly practically yanked the flowers out of her hands. "You really should get changed."

"Okay, okay." Had Spencer planned something special just for the two of them? She'd never taken him for the "big romantic gesture" type, but this could be fun. In that case, whatever event Joella had booked for this evening, she surely had everything under control and Lindsey could put it out of her mind.

Entering her room, she halted. Someone had laid out her new white sweater dress—the one she'd planned to wear next Saturday for her wedding. Next to the bed sat the floral embroidered cowgirl boots she'd found to match. A pink envelope peeked from the top of one of the boots.

She plucked out the envelope, her fingertips tingling as she withdrew the lacy, rhinestone-embellished Valentine's card. Opening it, she immediately recognized Spencer's lazy scrawl.

Welcome home, he'd written. *I know they say the groom shouldn't see the bride in her wedding dress before the ceremony, but please trust me. Pretend it's next Saturday and get dressed like you were planning. Then meet me at the chapel. I'll be the guy in the brand new shirt and jeans, white hat, and bolo tie. Oh, and bring those roses with you. All my love, Spencer.*

He wouldn't…would he? She went to the window and parted the curtains. It was impossible to see the chapel from this angle, but the backyard was aglow with twinkling white lights.

Someone tapped on her door, then opened it a crack.

"Linds?" It was Joella, who wore a calf-length gown of rose-colored velvet.

Holly slipped in behind her. She'd changed into a dress almost identical to Joella's. "Can we come in?"

"I think you'd better," Lindsey said with a one-eyed glare, "because somebody really needs to clue me in on what's going on."

Spencer paced the length of the chapel aisle, which, with his exaggerated strides, took only four steps in each direction. His hands were sweating, his heart was pounding, and with every step he prayed Lindsey wouldn't think he'd gone off his rocker but would soon walk through that door just like he'd envisioned a million times over the past few days.

On his next pass, Samuel snagged his arm. "Spiny, take a breath. She'll be here."

"I don't know…maybe this was too much." Pausing near the candlelit altar, he let his gaze roam the small, crowded room. It wasn't like he'd invited the whole town. Mom and Dad and Samuel—his best man, naturally. Lindsey's mother and stepdad had arrived last night. Audra had invited her closest friends from town, as had Mom and Dad. Holly and Joella had put out the word to a few other former classmates they'd kept in touch with, and three of them had driven in this afternoon. Aunt Alicia and Uncle David had sent their regrets and best wishes, along with a generous cash gift. Cousin Mark hadn't been able to break away from his job in Montana.

Also noticeably absent were Spencer's grandfather and Lindsey's dad. Probably a good thing. Tito hadn't raised any further objections to this marriage, but neither did he openly support it. At least he was on the mend physically. In the meantime, Spencer kept up his prayers for a once-and-forever end to the division between the Navarros and McClements.

He started pacing again.

When the chapel door swung open, he nearly jumped out of his skin.

Seeing it was only Joella, he whooshed out a breath that was part relief, part disappointment. He shot her a questioning stare.

"Relax, cowboy." Joella patted his arm. Her smile seemed to float over his shoulder in the direction of his twin before she focused back on him. "Obviously you have no idea how long it takes for a lady to get herself changed and gussied up after a couple of days at a smelly old cattle sale."

"So...she's coming down?"

"Any minute now." She winked. "And I promise, she's totally on board with the change of plans."

Nodding weakly, Spencer swallowed over the lump in his throat. Joella said something to the harpist, then exited through the double doors. As the strains of "The King of Love My Shepherd Is" wafted toward the rafters, the guests quieted.

Samuel's hands clamped down on Spencer's shoulders. "Better take your position. Looks like the festivities are about to begin."

He hauled in a breath and joined his brother in front of the altar. The pastor caught his eye and smiled.

Once again, the chapel doors opened. Holly's little boy entered, marching forward like a man on a mission. He carried a small white pillow with two gold rings secured in the center with satin ribbon. Holly came next, and then Joella, taking their places opposite Spencer and Samuel.

The harpist segued into "Be Thou My Vision," and suddenly Spencer's vision filled with the woman he couldn't wait to spend the rest of his life loving. His heart beat faster with every step Lindsey took toward him. Her eyes glistened with unshed tears, her smile as bright and full of hope as a springtime Texas sunrise.

The rest went by in a blur—the Scripture readings, the pastor's wedding homily, the vows, the exchange of rings, the pronouncement...

The kiss.

Afterward, the guests were invited to the house, where Holly had prepared a casual buffet supper of Tex-Mex favorites. With everyone spreading out through the living room, dining room and kitchen, Spencer found his coat and a shawl for his bride and coaxed her out to the front porch swing.

He snuggled her close. "Happy?"

"Unbelievably." She chuckled softly. "You are one surprising man, Mr. Navarro."

"In a good way, I hope."

"The best. One of these days you're going to have to tell me how you pulled this off without my knowing."

He laughed out loud. "With a *lot* of help, that's how!" Turning serious, he tilted her chin so he could gaze into her eyes. "If I were better with words, I'd have written my own vows. I'd have said you're the best thing that ever happened to me. I'd have said what a fool I was for ever letting you go. I'd have said that God blessed me a hundred times over when He brought you back into my life. I'd have said—"

She silenced him with a fingertip to his lips. "Spencer

Navarro, you really need to learn that there's a time for words, and there's a time for letting your kisses do the talking. Guess what time this is."

He didn't have to guess, because she wasted no time in showing him.

* * * * *

If you enjoyed The Rancher's Family Secret, *look for Myra Johnson's earlier books*

Rancher for the Holidays
Her Hill Country Cowboy
Hill Country Reunion
The Rancher's Redemption
Their Christmas Prayer

Available now from Love Inspired!
Find more great reads at www.LoveInspired.com

Dear Reader,

Maybe you've heard the saying, "You can choose your friends, but you can't choose your family." I suspect most families have at least one relative who requires an extra dose of patience, forbearance…and forgiveness. Unfortunately, it's far too easy to let others' negative attitudes infect us, even to the point of blaming God.

But God is always loving and wants only our very best. Remember, those "problem people" are God's children, too, and surely it grieves Him when their hurtful words or actions cause us distress. Also, as Spencer and Lindsey realized, we can't change the spiritual condition of anyone's heart but our own.

Instead, we can entrust our difficult relatives to God. The changes we pray for may not happen in our lifetime or theirs, but not forgiving is not an option. Forgiveness is a gift of healing and peace we give ourselves in obedience to God's word: "And be ye kind one to another, tenderhearted, forgiving one another, even as God for Christ's sake hath forgiven you" (Ephesians 4:32, KJV).

I hope Spencer and Lindsey's story has touched or inspired you. I love to hear from readers, so please contact me through my website, MyraJohnson.com, where you can also subscribe to my e-newsletter. Or you can write to me c/o Love Inspired Books, 195 Broadway, 24th Floor, New York, NY 10007.

With prayers and gratitude,
Myra

WE HOPE YOU ENJOYED
THIS BOOK FROM

LOVE INSPIRED
INSPIRATIONAL ROMANCE

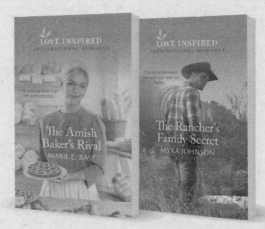

Uplifting stories of faith, forgiveness and hope.

Fall in love with stories where faith helps
guide you through life's challenges, and discover
the promise of a new beginning.

6 NEW BOOKS AVAILABLE EVERY MONTH!

SOMEONE TO TRUST
North Country Amish • by Patricia Davids

Esther Burkholder has no interest in her stepmother's matchmaking when her family visits an Amish community in Maine. Deaf since she was eight, she's positive a hearing man couldn't understand the joys and trials of living in a silent world. But Amish bachelor Gabe Fisher might just change her mind...

HER FORBIDDEN AMISH LOVE
by Jocelyn McClay

After her sister's departure to the *Englisch* world, Hannah Lapp couldn't hurt her parents by leaving, too—so she ended her relationship with the Mennonite man she'd hoped to marry. Now Gabe Bartel's back in her life... and this time, she's not so sure she can choose her community over love.

CHOOSING HIS FAMILY
Colorado Grooms • by Jill Lynn

Rescuing a single mom and her triplets during a snowstorm lands rancher Finn Brightwood with temporary tenants in his vacation rental. But with his past experiences, Finn's reluctant to get too involved in Ivy Darling's chaotic life. So why does he find himself wishing this family would stick around for good?

HIS DRY CREEK INHERITANCE
Dry Creek • by Janet Tronstad

When he returns home after receiving a letter from his foster father, soldier Mark Dakota learns that the man has recently passed away. Now in order to get his share of the inheritance, Mark must temporarily help his foster brother's widow, Bailey Rosen, work the ranch. But can he avoid falling for his childhood friend?

A HOME FOR HER BABY
by Gabrielle Meyer

Forced to sell her bed-and-breakfast, Piper Connelly's happy to stay on as manager—until the pregnant widow discovers her former high school sweetheart, Max Evans, is the buyer. While Max has grown from the boy who once broke her heart, is giving him a second chance worth the risk?

AN UNLIKELY PROPOSAL
by Toni Shiloh

When Trinity Davis is laid off, her best friend, Omar Young, proposes a solution to all their problems—a marriage of convenience. After all, that would provide her much-needed health insurance and give the widower's little girls a mother. And they'll never have to risk their bruised hearts again...